Lenharrow
Badd Company Chronicles
Book 8
"The Shadow Knights"

By
Mr. & Mrs. Christopher Hildt
"Logan & Tyger"

Table of Contents

Chapter #	Book 8
0	Falbar's Prologue
1	The Mystery Man
2	The Strange Book
3	Secrets Revealed
4	Nobody Wants to Stay Behind
5	Winged Attack
6	The Home Front
7	Trouble on the Way
8	The Way In
9	The Siege
10	The Council Meeting
11	Deceptions

Falbar's Prologue

On our last adventure we were drug into a
plot by a dangerous Spider Cult and although
our company now numbered eight persons we were
joined by two mysterious elves who were
friends of Martin's from Plenty that were
seeking our help for some reason.

Unfortunately, our current task had to be
completed first so the two of them, a noble
elf maid and her strong and powerful brother,
joined us on that outing. They proved to be
valuable companions in our fight against the
bandits and then the Spider Cult itself.

We arrived in Torrenth and discovered
that people were missing and that they were
being taken right out of their own homes in
the middle of the night. We did a little
investigating but before we were able to
really get into it the elf maid who called
herself Shaldra took off without a word and
for some reason Martin went after her by
himself. Dee had Eric gathered up the rest of
the company as he hurried after our half-elven
companion. We followed as quickly as we were
able but before we could reach them they had
all been captured by the bandits. Clint
tracked our foes to their hideout but by the
time we had found our friends Synbadd pretty
much had things already under control. We
found a magical gateway in the bandits'
hideout but instead of going blindly into a
situation Dee decided that we all should
return to Torrenth and get some
reinforcements. With a small detachment of
troops we returned to the hideout but there
was no sign of more bandits as we feared so
Mozart used a key Mitch had found but it did
not seem to open the gateway until Derrkon
pointed out that the gateway looked dwarven

and that perhaps the key was actually designed to be used backwards. It worked like a charm and the portal opened up so as we often do, the Badd Company pressed forward into the unknown.

Beyond the portal we found a labyrinth that our foes felt we could not possibly find our way through. At the end of the maze, however, we were attacked by a hideous spider-like fiend. Even with all of our experience and skill the creature nearly defeated us, in the end however, Derrkon slew what we learned later to be a spider hound. Sadly, most of us were in no shape to defend ourselves and were easily captured by the Spider Cult and their minions.

We were in captivity once again but this time we escaped on our own and finally confronted the mastermind behind the cult. It was a harrowing battle as most of them are but this time we were seriously hard pressed to win the day. We were all badly wounded and after we'd bested our foes we returned to Torrenth and found it under attack by the remaining bandits and their wily Spiderian leader. We rescued the town once more and Synbadd dispatched the Spiderian with great satisfaction saving my life in the same breath.

After staying over to help Torrenth recover somewhat we then rushed back to Haven's Run as Clint and Shaldra had been infected with a terrible curse but the Gnomish Healers easily remedied their maladies and after a much needed rest we all decided that it was time to help our two new elven friends and it appeared that our bout with shadow was about to continue but first questions needed answering; questions that hung in the air like insistent gnats. Martin had been hiding things from us and we hoped he could finally trust us with his secrets that obviously involved Shaldra and her companion that was more of a bodyguard than a brother. Dee had promised to help her and that meant that the Badd Company was needed once again but with a problem this large who else would answer the call as we prepared to do battle with…

"The Shadow Knights"

Chapter 1
"The Mystery Man"

It was night in the city of Haven's Run and the streets were slightly wet from rain but it had stopped for quite some time. Most of the people that live there were either at home in bed or sitting in one of the many taverns in the city. Very few people roamed the streets this late at night but one man did. He was looking for a particular house and he was completely lost. The human man stood at 5'8" with dirty brown hair and cunning blue eyes that searched frantically for his destination. He wore an old suit of scratched up leather and he had a half rusted short sword at his side. A dark green cloak covered his grizzled features and he held an object in his arms that was covered in black velvet. His eyes darted from side to side watching for danger as he tried to avoid being seen but that was not to be.

"You there, what are you up to?" A town guardsman stopped him.

"Nothing, good sir." The man bowed slightly.

"What have you got in your hands?" The guard demanded.

"It's just a gift for an old friend of mine." He replied.

"Oh yeah let me see that?" The guard held out his hand.

There was only one guard and the man had half a mind to punch the guy out cold and run but that was shattered as two more guards appeared out of nowhere.

"What's going on here?" One of the newcomers asked.

"This man is refusing to reveal what he carries." The first man reported.

"Well then we must confiscate the object then." The second newcomer suggested.

"Hardly reason enough to harass a man," the second guard stated.

"Look good sirs it really is nothing." The cloaked man explained.

"Then you won't mind if we see it now will you?" The original guard tried to grab at the object.

The cloaked figure drew back and tried to run but one of the guards tripped him as he broke through. He fell to the floor and the object that he protected for so long went flying across the dirt road. When he saw one of the guards picking up the object he quickly withdrew a small key from his neck and stuffed it in his sock. Thankfully none of them saw him do this so the key remained unknown.

"Well what have we here?" The man removed the cloth to reveal an ornately decorated book.

"What is that?" One of the others asked.

"Looks like a stolen book from the school of magic." The guard replied.

"No sir. I was taking that book to Lord Dee Bridges." The man explained as he got up off the floor.

"A likely story. Arrest him." He ordered the other two men.

"No I swear that book belongs to Lord Dee Bridges!" The man shouted as the guards took him away.

"We'll just see about that in the morning." He said as he walked away and the man was taken to the local jailhouse.

Not too far away inside a tavern called Four Star Falbar's a tall handsome man sits upon a stage strumming a lute and singing a song. He's 6'2" with wavy brown hair and sparkling brown eyes that compliment his handsome face. He wore a frilly white long sleeved shirt and a pair of blue-green breeches with a shiny blue sash. His voice was like a thousand angels and he held his audience captive, especially the ladies. A shower of roses was thrown at his feet as he finished and several encores were shouted throughout the room.

"Please ladies and gentlemen that was my third encore." The minstrel bowed as he stepped down.

Disappointment filled the room but the mood lightened as a pair of acrobats took the stage. The man strode purposefully to a table where four men, three elves, a half-elf, and one dwarf already sat. Several of the ladies that were sitting on the table in front of the stage followed him.

"May we join you Falbar?" A woman dressed in red asked.

"Um, I don't know. Dee?" He looked at a bearded man with black hair.

He had piercing blue eyes and stood at six feet tall. The man wore a suit of chain mail with the familiar red tunic of Haven's Run covering it. At his belt, hung a short sword and a broad sword with his family crest; marking him as a nobleman. His brown hood was pulled back so you could see his short black hair framing a handsome young face. He is also known as Synbadd which means heroic officer of the guard in the dwarvish language.

"You took so long with your performance that we already discussed our business." Dee told Falbar.

"And?" The minstrel wondered.

"We haven't found what we've been looking for." The noble responded.

"Well then it appears that the rest of the evening can be enjoyed. Ladies?" He pulled out one of the chairs and the woman in red sat down.

"Wait, oh well." Dee threw up his hands.

"It can't be helped now Dee. Hello miss." A handsome young elf turned to one of the women at the table.

He was 5'6" with long yet neatly combed soft brown hair and dark blue eyes that hid an unknown secret. He wore long purple robes that were tied at the waist with a shining golden belt and a battle axe was at his side. The elf was a mage by trade and it was evident by how he spoke.

"Hi, you're cute. What's your name?" The woman sitting next to him greeted.

"Mozart Martakamis." He replied with a bow.

"I really don't get what these women see in that peacock." A human soldier sulked as he looked at the ladies fawning all over Falbar.

He was 5'11" tall with short dirty unkempt light brown hair and wild looking brown eyes. He wore dark brown tanned armor, a red Haven's Run tunic, a bright long sword, and a rather plain looking short sword.

"You're just jealous because none of them are interested in you, Clint." A young man that looked similar to him said.

This man was 5'9" with short slightly neater brown hair and cunning brown eyes that were constantly searching for danger. He was wearing worn leather armor and a dark green cloak with a well sharpened long sword and a battle axe at his belt.

"You should talk Mitch; you've never even been with a woman." Clint teased.

"Just because he didn't spend all his money on a prostitute as soon as his manhood dropped doesn't mean you need to tease him." A boy that shared the same features as the other two spoke up.

This boy was 5'7" and had short flaming red hair and clear light brown eyes that were filled with wonder. He wore soft brown leather armor with the red tunic of Haven's Run and a long sword at his side.

"Thanks for the support bro." Mitch smiled at him.

"Like you got…" Clint was cut short.

"Now you leave young Eric alone. After all he's only sixteen." The dwarf interrupted.

He was a stout 4'5" brown haired dwarf that had two braids neatly tied in his beard and dark brown eyes that had a certain joy in them. He wore shining iron armor trimmed in blue and silver. He had two battle axes at his side and a shield bearing the symbol of the House of Rockbeard denoting his nobility.

"So I was fourteen." The soldier shot back.

"I agree with Lord Rockbeard." Another elf piped in.

He was 5'2" with short brown hair and blue-grey eyes that foretold of the many battles he witnessed. His shiny steel armor was covered by a black cloak and he had a finely crafted elven sword at his side. Along his chest was a bandolier filed with several hand axes that could easily be removed and thrown at a moments notice.

"You would Rydol." Clint responded glumly as everyone seemed against him.

"No thank you, miss. As a priest of The Bright One I do not partake in such activities." The half-elf spoke up.

He was a handsome 5'4" man that was more elven looking than human and he had short blonde hair with innocent blue eyes that had a kind of peace in them. He wore the familiar white robes of a priest of a god who was just known as The Bright One. The robes were accented with yellow trim and a symbol of a big yellow circle was emblazoned on his chest. A beautiful white mace that gave off a holy aura hung on a hook at his belt and a shield was slung over his back.

"Aww come on Martin. How can you keep denying your manly urges?" Clint complained as he watched the priest decline a beautiful woman's offer to sleep with him.

At that remark the last of the company that sat at the table originally, got up and left the tavern. She was the only female in the party and she stood at 4'7" with long flowing red hair and bright green eyes that shone like emeralds. Her beautiful elven features were enough to turn any man's head as she walked by. She wore finely crafted steel armor that was form fitted to her and had gold trim etched on it. A long green cloak flowed behind her that parted at the top to reveal a long bow and a quiver full of specially made arrows. At her belt was a bright elven sword sheathed in a scabbard decorated with elvish runes. When she left the tavern Martin shot Clint an angry glare before getting up to follow her and Mitch hit him on the shoulder.

"Oww, what was that for?" He looked at his brother.

"You know how Martin feels about
Shaldra." Falbar scolded him.

"No, what are you talking about?" The
soldier turned to the minstrel.

"You mean you haven't noticed?" Eric
broke in.

"Noticed what?" Clint looked around
confused.

"The way he looks at her and how he takes
extra care of her. You know stuff like that."
Falbar explained but when Clint still had a
look of confusion on his face he turned to the
elven soldier. "You know what I'm talking
about right Rydol?"

"No I don't." The elf looked at Clint and
the two of them just shrugged.

The truth was that Rydol knew exactly
what they were talking about but he couldn't
let anyone else know. Shaldra was supposed to
be his sister when in truth she was Vandrossa
Birchbark the Queen of Plenty and he was her
captain of the guard. He wasn't worried about
the looks Martin was giving her either because
the two were married, a secret that all who
knew it had to keep. It was a well known fact
in the company that assassins were after the
priest but they all thought that it was
because of his family which was not wholly
true. Plenty is a matriarchal society and when
the queen got married someone wanted to stop
her from producing an heir so they are trying
to kill her husband. He fled to Haven's Run to
grow strong enough to protect her and the
family they wish to start. Martin decided to
join his wife outside and noted that the
cobblestones on the street were still quite
wet.

"I'm sorry about that." The noble priest
apologized.

"It's alright, I know they mean well." She looked into his eyes.

"Perhaps but it can be very trying sometimes." He admitted.

"I love you Martin." Vandrossa suddenly grabbed her husband and kissed him passionately.

"Vandrossa, someone might see us." The half-elf pulled away.

"I'm sorry; it's just that I'm tired of hiding in the shadows. I long for the days that we were able to spend in Plenty. I want to be able to shout to the world that you're my husband. I …" She stopped as tears formed in her eyes.

"Don't worry my love all will be well soon enough." Martin held her in his arms.

The reason she had to leave her country and join him in Haven's Run was because the capital was seized by powerful creatures called Shadow Lords. She and Rydol were barely able to escape but it didn't come without a price. The Queen was violated by a powerful wizard and a deep elf so Martin had to take special care of her. The evil deed nearly tore the two of them apart but in the end they were able to sort things out.

"What if someone sees us like this?" She asked as she buried her face in his chest.

"Let them, we're going to have to tell them the truth sooner or later." He answered as he bent down to kiss her but they were interrupted by the sound of footsteps.

"Lord Tierleaf, is Lord Bridges inside?" A soldier recognized the priest as one of Dee's entourage.

"Yes, he is." Martin told him and the three of them went inside.

"Well I say he can't do it!" Clint was shouting at Falbar.

"Ten gold says I can." The minstrel responded.

"Lord Bridges." The approaching soldier bowed to the nobleman.

"Yes Corporal?" Dee raised an eyebrow.

"Captain Roberts asked me to inform you that he has arrested someone tonight that claims to have something belonging to you." The soldier reported.

"Inform the captain that I will visit him in the morning." The nobleman ordered.

"What's that all about?" Clint wondered.

"Don't know, want to come along?" Dee asked.

"Oh yeah; most definitely." The soldier responded eagerly.

Chapter 2
"The Strange Book"

Todd Coalman sat in his tiny cell contemplating the many events that ultimately led him here. He was a coal miner as was his father and his grandfather. He came from a long line of coal miners; it was hard work but honest at least that's what his father always told him. His mother died when he was very young and he never knew what happened to her as his father rarely spoke of her. He had no siblings and the only members of his family that he knew were his father and his uncle. The three of them mined in the town of Dover. However, Torrenth had been the town of his birth and after his mother's death they'd been forced to move to Dover that is until there was a collapse in the mine killing his father and uncle. He found himself alone for the first time and he wasn't sure what to do so he took the last of his money and traveled to Haven's Run to find work. However they had no mines so he had to try to find some other kind of work. He tried doing other things like running messages, cleaning clothes, and even shining boots but none of those jobs made enough money for him to survive on. One day a man came to him about a job but it wasn't honest work and at first Todd turned him down. After a few days went by and no other jobs came up he became desperate so he went back to the man. He thought that he would do just one job for this guy just to get by and then he would never see him again. However greed got the better of him as he made more money in one day for one job then he would working several jobs in one week.

Crime became second nature to the man; he started with petty theft which led to grand theft. He later joined a gang and started committing other types of crimes like extortion, skullduggery, and eventually murder. The last one he never really liked doing but things happened and people get in the way. It probably would still be the same today if it weren't for his last job. An evil Spiderian hired everyone in his gang to kidnap people in his old town. He had grown to hate that town for what happened to his family so he thought he was getting a little bit of vengeance. Unfortunately, once he found out what they were doing with the people it was too late; he was in too deep. Luckily he found his opportunity to escape when a group of adventurers took down the evil cult he worked for and the Spiderian that hired him. On his way out he ran into the leader of this company and he thought that it was the end of his life but the man showed mercy on him and let him leave in peace. Todd swore that he would find out the man's name and repay him somehow but he wasn't sure what he could do. It was easy enough to find out that the man that spared him was Trade Commissioner Lord Dee Bridges but finding out what he could do to help him was a little more difficult. He didn't think that the nobleman would accept him the way he was so he followed around the members of his entourage.

Several days went by as he followed different members of the company and all he figured out was they were looking for something. It wasn't until he followed the elven conjurer into the magic school library that he got a hint of what they wanted. He knew that they would not find any answers in the city of Haven's Run so he went to the one place that did: Torrenth. After obtaining that which he sought he returned to the capital. Now he was back and even though he knew where Lord Bridges lived he got lost in the darkness and ultimately arrested. He leaned back on the wall and looked up at the ceiling which appeared dark and foreboding. Hopefully he'll be able to explain things to the nobleman before he does as he promised and slays him for committing one more crime.

It was early morning and Dee had somewhere to go but first he had to wake his friend which was going to be fun since they stayed up so long. He crept silently into Clint's room even though the soldier was snoring loud enough to wake the dead. He took out his short sword and held it at the man's throat.

"Don't even move." He warned.

The sleeping man surprised the nobleman as his legs swung up and grabbed Dee by the head. He went flying across the room and the soldier was instantly upon him with a dagger in his hands.

"Oh good morning Dee! Is it time to go?" Clint yawned.

The nobleman kicked the soldier's feet out from beneath him and disarmed the man in one swift move. He then flipped him over and held Clint's hands behind his back so that he couldn't move.

"Give up?" Dee teased.

"Never!" The soldier shouted as his head flung back and hit the nobleman's hands away.

Clint twisted underneath him grabbed his head with his legs again and flung Dee backwards. The two men were on their feet

instantly and the soldier found his dagger in
his hands once more.

"I think mine's bigger." Dee looked down
at his short sword.

"It's not the size that counts." Clint
lunged forward and caught the nobleman's
shoulder.

Dee took the hit and twisted to allow the
man to go past him then he grabbed his arm to
hold it behind his back. The nobleman threw
Clint into the wall and placed his free hand
behind his neck, pinning him down. The soldier
wiggled around trying to free himself but
Dee's hold was just too good for him.

"Alright you can let go now." The man
surrendered.

"Say it." Dee demanded.

"No way man!" Clint denied him.

"I said say it." The nobleman pushed him
into the wall.

"OK, OK, you win. Are you happy?" He
shouted.

"Is that all?" Dee was playing with him.

"You got me already! What more do you
want?" The soldier squirmed about like a worm
on a hook.

"Nothing, mom's got breakfast ready so
hurry up." The nobleman laughed as he let the
man go.

Clint walked over to his dagger and
picked it up off of the floor. He half wanted
to start up the fight again but remembered why
they were up so early in the morning. He
smiled to himself as he thought of the fun
that was sure to come and he put the dagger
away.

Dee left the man to get ready as he
walked downstairs and was surprised to see
Derrkon, Martin, and Mozart in the kitchen.

His mother was serving them pancakes with sausage and fresh orange juice. The rest of his family was asleep at this hour and Dee hoped to sneak out without much fuss but that was not to be.

"Good morning everyone," Dee greeted.

"Good morning son. Ahhh, what's happened to your arm?" His mother screamed as she looked at the bleeding cut that Clint caused.

"It's nothing mother. Clint and I were just playing around." He told her.

"That is an awfully large wound for just playing around. Something like that could be dangerous if not healed properly." Martin said as he examined the nobleman's arm and then healed it quickly as he saw Lady Bridges' eyes grow big.

"You two need to be more careful and quit playing like that in the house, you hear me?" She scolded her son.

"Yes mother." Dee sighed as he sat at the table.

"I mean it son, you're not too big for me to take you over my knee." She looked at him sternly.

"That's right Lady E. Kick his tubb." Clint said as he walked into the kitchen.

"You too Clint, I don't want to see anymore wounds like that on either of you from just playing around." She pointed a spatula at the soldier.

"Yes, Lady E." The soldier cringed and hung his head as he went to the breakfast table.

"So why is everyone up so early?" Dee asked as he turned to his companions.

"It's Salutation." Derrkon informed the Commander.

"Oh, church day." Clint rolled his eyes.

"Just because you don't attend church doesn't mean you have to demean those that do." Mozart chided.

"What about you Mozart? The school is closed today and I don't believe I have ever seen you attend any services." Martin wondered.

"Well, I just happen to know the librarian quite well and she's going to make a special exception on my behalf." The conjurer smiled slyly.

"I see." The noble priest blushed slightly as Mozart looked directly at him.

"And where are you off to Clint?" Derrkon asked.

"Dee and I got a prisoner to interrogate." He smiled broadly at the dwarf.

"We're not going to rough him up Clint, just question him." Dee got up from the table as he wiped his mouth.

"Of course not." The soldier winked at the table as he grabbed a piece of toast and followed his commander.

The two men walked silently through the streets to Captain Roberts' guardhouse and were greeted by the same corporal from last night. He looked like he had been there all night and was ready to go home to get some sleep. He smiled sheepishly at the nobleman and then escorted him and his companion to the captain's office.

"Greetings Lord Bridges." A big man stood up from behind a desk.

"So what seems to be the problem captain?" Dee asked as he sat down. Clint on the other hand folded his arms and leaned against the wall behind his commander.

"Well I have a man here who claims this book belongs to you." He pulled out a finely decorated book that was bound with a keyed latch out of a drawer.

"I have a small library at home but none of the books are this exotic." The nobleman picked up the book to examine it.

"I didn't think so. My men believe he stole it from the school of magic and I was going to check that out after I spoke with you." The captain explained.

"Did the prisoner give a name?" Dee inquired as he handed the book back.

"He says his name is Todd Coalman. Do you know him?" He said.

"Never heard of him," the nobleman confirmed the soldier's suspicions.

"I didn't believe that either. Do you want to question him?" Captain Roberts wondered.

"Most definitely," Dee replied.

"He's in cell number four." The man stood up and handed a key to the nobleman.

"Thanks." He took the key and left the office.

"What do you think?" Clint asked as they went to the dungeon in the jailhouse.

"I don't know but I don't think that book came from the magic school." Dee told his friend.

"How do you figure?" The soldier was confused.

"A couple of things; first he was arrested by Four Star Falbar's." He said.

"So?" Clint opened the door to the cell block.

"So the school of magic is by the palace and if he was looking for my house he was coming from the wrong direction and second why would someone steal a book and then hand it to the Trade Commissioner?" Dee explained.

"Good point. That's why you're the brains
of this outfit and I'm the muscle." The
soldier admitted.

The two men stopped at the iron door that
had a red four painted on the outside and Dee
took out the large key while Clint picked up
one of the torches on the wall in the hall.
The nobleman opened the door to reveal a
sleeping man lying on the floor and the
soldier ran in swords drawn. He picked up the
man who woke up immediately and pressed his
weapon against the prisoner's throat.

"Clint what are you doing?" Dee demanded.

"This is one of those spider bandits from
Torrenth and the exact one you let go with the
warning that you would slay him for any
crime!" The soldier shouted.

"I'm not so sure he's committed a crime
so let's hear his side of the story before we
go around killing the man." The nobleman
ordered and Clint complied as he put him down.

"Thank you Lord Bridges" The man bowed.

"Who are you and what do you want with
me?" Dee glared at him.

"My name's Todd Coalman my lord and I was
bringing you something that your friends have
been searching for." He answered.

"The guards claim you stole that book."
The nobleman accused.

"I'm afraid they're right but not from
where they say. You see my lord I stole that
book from my former employer." Todd explained.

"What is it?" Dee had to hold back his
young friend from advancing again.

"The key to the Shadow Knights' defeat"

The nobleman flinched at the words. "How
did you know that we were looking for this
information?" He wondered.

"I'm sad to say that I've been following your friends to see what I could do to help you for sparing my life. I meant no harm my lord. You've been the only man I ever met that showed me kindness and I am truly grateful." Todd bowed again.

"If your story proves true then you will be released. I'll have a friend of mine examine the contents of the book and then…" He was cut off.

"Begging your lordships pardon but the book is magically held shut and to open it without the key could prove fatal." The man warned.

"Let me guess, you're the only one that knows where this key is." Dee surmised.

"Yes." He answered.

"And you won't give it to me without getting you out of here right?" The nobleman asked.

"I'll get him to tell us where it is!" Clint pulled out his short sword again and held it up menacingly.

"No my lord, I give it to you freely with hopes that you will help me." The man pulled the small golden key out of his sock and handed it to Dee.

"How do I know this is the real key and not some kind of trap?" The nobleman looked at it skeptically.

"Why would I have warned you about the book and then hand you the key if it was a trap?" Todd shot back.

"Good point." He replied.

"One more thing my lord there is a chant that you must speak before opening the lock otherwise the creature will get away." The man told him.

"What creature?" Dee looked at him with confusion.

"Why the Shadow Knight trapped inside of course." Todd answered and both men dropped their jaws in shock.

Chapter 3
"Secrets Revealed"

Dee thought it was only right to get Todd released especially since he didn't commit any recent crimes. It was confirmed that the book didn't come from the magic school unfortunately the former bandit was wanted for other crimes against Haven's Run. The nobleman ordered that Todd's punishment should be service under him and the man was all too happy to agree to his sentence. Dee and Clint immediately went over to the school of magic to look for Mozart but he wasn't there. Luckily, a student from the school happened to see him leave the library with the librarian early that morning. Dee suspected that the conjurer went to her house so he asked the student where she lived. He hated to interrupt Mozart and his new companion but this was really important. The three men walked down the street where they were directed only to see the elf leaving a small house. He was with a beautiful young lady with long strawberry blonde hair, ruby lips, and devilishly enticing green eyes. Dee hailed the conjurer and he waved in response.

"Dee, what are you doing here?" Mozart asked as the nobleman came up to him.

"Looking for you… Am I interrupting something?" He smiled slyly.

"Actually we were about to go to lunch. What do you need?" The conjurer held the woman's hand.

"There has been an interesting development regarding our latest endeavor and I need you to help me out right now." Synbadd explained.

"Oh, well it looks like I'm needed elsewhere Darcy. I will have to meet with you some other time." He kissed her hand gently.

"I'll be waiting for you." She pulled the conjurer towards her and kissed him passionately.

"Whoa, if I would've known that the librarian was that hot I think I would have learned to read instead of wield a sword." Clint said after they walked for a little bit.

"Yeah, so are you and Darcy serious Mozart?" Dee asked.

"Nah we're just enjoying each others company. Why, you interested?" The mage pulled back the loose hair in his face.

"Perhaps" The nobleman replied.

"So what's this new development?" Mozart wondered.

"It's best said indoors if you know what I mean. I was wondering if you could send messages to the others to meet at my house as soon as possible." Dee asked.

"Easily done," he replied as he started to conjure.

"Oh and tell them it's very important." Dee added.

Half an hour later the whole company, except Eric and Mitch who had other duties to attend to, were in Dee's lounge wondering what was so important. Dee and Derrkon held a large mug of Bridges Ale while Clint leaned back on a chair with his feet up on a small table. Falbar was glaring at the soldier for he knew that Mrs. B hated it when feet were put on her furniture and Mozart smiled to himself for he enjoyed the tension between the two men. Martin kept glancing at the doorway nervously

while the company waited patiently for his
wife and her bodyguard.

"I'm sorry for taking so long Dee but I
was in the middle of a ceremony of succession
when I received your note." Vandrossa walked
into the room with Rydol.

"That's alright but what exactly is a
ceremony of succession?" The nobleman
wondered.

"It's a ceremony held for those that have
gained a higher power. Congratulations
Shaldra, we're proud of you." Derrkon smiled
as he hit Martin on the shoulder.

"Whoop de do." Clint spun his finger in
the air.

"I'll remember that the next time you get
cursed Clint." She smiled at him devilishly.

"Dear lady, I sincerely apologize for my
rude remark." The soldier bent down suddenly
and kissed her hand.

"Get off her you filthy letch." Falbar
kicked him over as he knew the only reason he
was apologizing was to get the chance to kiss
the elven woman.

"Oh, you wanna fight toch? Come on."
Clint challenged as he put up his fists.

"Sit down right now both of you!" Dee
demanded and Falbar sat quickly as Clint eyed
him fiercely.

"I said now Clint." The nobleman glared
at him.

"What is all this about Dee?" Mozart
asked ignoring the angry men glowering at each
other.

"A fascinating artifact has fallen into
my hands and I'm going to need each of you to
help me figure it out." Dee started.

"What kind of artifact?" The conjurer
leaned forward with interest.

"A book that somehow holds a Shadow Lord inside of it, or better yet: A shadow knight" The room suddenly became quiet and all eyes were upon their commander.

"Did you just say what I think you said?" Derrkon broke the silence.

"Yes I'm afraid so." Dee answered.

"How is this possible?" Vandrossa wondered "And what do you mean by Shadow Knight?"

"I'm not sure but we can use this to our advantage. The problem is where are we going to open it to find out its weaknesses?" The nobleman inquired of the group.

"The magic school?" Mozart offered.

"No. There are too many people there just in case something goes wrong." He informed the conjurer.

"What's wrong with here?" Clint waved his arms about.

"Are you kidding? My mother would kill all of us." Dee rejected the idea immediately.

"How about the palace? Archduchess Shazaron did offer to help us and I'm sure she'll have a secure place for us to work." Vandrossa offered.

"Good idea Shaldra. Let's go get Todd and the book and head over to the palace." Dee stood up and headed for the front door.

"Who's Todd?" Falbar wondered.

"The guy who brought me the book and hopefully a new friend," the nobleman answered.

Everyone followed Dee outside and was amazed at what they saw. Paris, the wolf Synbadd raised, was on top of a scruffy looking man licking his face. The wolf didn't like strangers especially when they are on

Dee's property so it was a surprise to see him get along so famously with the unknown man.

"Well I see that you met Paris." Dee said as he approached the two.

"He's a fine animal my lord." Todd got up and bowed to the nobleman.

"If you're going to work for me then you should know one thing. Never call me 'milord'. Dee or Synbadd is just fine." He put his hand on the man's shoulder.

Dee quickly introduced his company to Todd and he pulled the book out of a piece of black velvet. Mozart immediately took the book and looked at it in amazement as he explained the rarity of it. The only one that was truly interested in his explanation was Falbar but that wasn't surprising since he loved all kinds of ancient lore especially when it involved magic. The elf returned the book to Todd and the company was soon on their way to the palace.

"Synbadd! What brings you to my palace on this fine day?" A tall voluptuous rust colored cat woman greeted as they entered the throne room.

She stood at 8'6" with seductive green eyes and she wore a long black skirt, a very revealing black top, and a bright red cloak clasped with a ruby amulet. At her belt was an impressive looking war hammer that seemed to hum with power. Behind her a black wolf woman by the name of Captain Marta Woolfe standing at an impressive 8'4" with cunning golden eyes that sparkled with a kind of playfulness. She wore finely crafted chain armor over a sleek yet powerful body and the familiar red tunic of Haven's Run with a lightning bolt on the black side of the shield. An elegant cutlass hung from her belt in a black leather sheath and she fingered the pommel as the company approached. It wasn't the company that made her nervous but the stranger that they brought with them for he was unfamiliar to her.

"Your grace I come with a special request that is best said in private." Dee bowed low before the cat woman.

"Really? Just you and me alone?" She rubbed her claw along his ear playfully.

"Me and my company Archduchess" He swallowed hard.

"Are you sure?" Shazaron smiled slyly.

"Yes my liege." He bowed once more.

"Very well, you may all follow me." She looked at the whole company before she turned and walked away.

They followed her through a door and she walked over to the wall and pressed a stone into it. Suddenly, a stone panel opened up to reveal a dark tunnel that lit up as soon as she walked into the hall. The wolf woman followed directly behind her and the rest of the company after that. The hall opened up into a large fifty foot square room that had a round table in the center surrounded by several chairs. It was a war room of sorts only this one was protected from any kind of spying including by magical means.

"So what do you need my friend?" Shazaron asked as she sat lazily in one of the chairs.

"A safe place to open this" Dee took the book from Todd and placed it on the table.

"What is it?" Her nose started to twitch as she sniffed the air.

"You want to explain it Todd?" He turned to look at the man.

"Um if you wish my lord," Todd said sheepishly.

"Don't worry she doesn't bite, hard." The nobleman smiled and he relaxed slightly.

"Well my liege it holds a Shadow Knight inside." He started to explain.

"You're not letting that thing loose in my palace." She pushed the book away as if it was about to bite her.

"You need not worry about it getting loose your majesty for I know the chant that keeps it trapped within a magical circle." Todd tried to reassure her.

"Oh well in that case here is good." She waved her hand to indicate the room they were standing in.

"Are you sure about that my lady? Perhaps you should not be in here when I open the book for they are quite frightful and you may…" The cat woman cut him off.

"I fear nothing!" She growled.

"I apologize I meant nothing by it my liege." He cowered before her and she placed a gentle hand on his shoulder.

"All will be alright with so many handsome warriors here with me I'm sure I'll be well protected. Wouldn't you say Dee?" She smiled sweetly at him.

"Yes Shazaron. Go ahead Todd we're ready for this." He pulled out his broad sword just in case.

The company helped to move the large table out of the way as Todd placed the book on the floor. He pulled out the small golden key from a bag on his belt and put it in the keyhole. The man chanted strange words from a long since dead language and a red circle formed around the book. He then turned the key and slowly walked out of the circle.

"Open." Todd said and the book complied.

A cold aura came out of the tome as well as a darkness that gave everyone a shiver down their spine. A black, shadowy creature that was neither living nor dead stood up and floated towards the barrier. It pulled out a nasty looking jagged long sword and tried to attack the man that commanded the book to open. A wall of red light shot up from the circle and it was as if the shadowed figure hit a magical barrier. It screeched in anger and a cold terror filled the hearts of everyone there. Vandrossa grabbed Martin's hand and he squeezed it in reassurance for he could tell that she was shaking with fear. The Queen of Plenty remembered how these creatures suddenly appeared in her palace and slaughtered many elves before she fled the capital. She remembered the words of their leader warning the people that they would kill the council, their families, and the Queen if they didn't do as he commanded. Vandrossa figured that someone in the council posed as her and she was able to escape to find help. Unfortunately, she couldn't go to any of her allies for everyone in Clinton would surely be slain if an army approached the woods.

"Oh yeah, I sense the undead. Let's go kill it my friend." A voice called from Clint's sword and he looked at Dee who looked at Todd.

"You can do as you please my lord. The beast cannot leave the circle nor can it attack anyone out here. My former employers were trying to discover the creature's secrets so they designed the circle to give anyone who entered it a kind of protection. I will show you how it works." The man explained and as he entered the circle a red aura surrounded him and the creature could do nothing to harm him.

"Cool." Clint said as he pulled his sword
free and entered the circle as Todd left.

"Ouch, what is that?" The sword shouted
as it hit the corrupted creature.

"Are you alright Tecklar?" The soldier
asked.

"Yes but that's no ordinary undead. I'm
not doing anything to hurt it." The sword
replied and Clint exited the magical barrier.

"Alright, who wants to try something
next?" Dee asked as he looked around the
party.

"I guess I'll give it a go." Mozart said
as he started to conjure before he entered the
magical circle.

The elf tried every spell that he knew of
and nothing seemed to do anything to the
beast. It hissed at him as if laughing and it
only served to fuel the elf's rage. He pulled
out his axe and attacked the creature to no
avail. The company tried many things like
different weapons, some magical some not.
Martin tried different types of divine spells
but nothing happened and the company was
getting discouraged. The hours in the day
waned and Shazaron suggested that they break
for dinner. The company agreed and they all
adjourned to the dinning hall for a grand
meal. They were all in a disheartened mood so
Falbar took out his lute to play a cheerful
tune and the company soon forgot about their
failures.

Vandrossa, on the other hand, could only
remember the darkness that dwelled within her
capital city and the horrors she left behind.
Not feeling like being cheered up she left the
company and went to feel the coolness of the
night air. Rydol got up to follow her when he
was stopped by Martin and the soldier

understood. The nobleman wanted to be the one
to comfort his wife and Rydol wasn't about to
stop him so he joined in the party's
merriment. It took a while for the elf to get
used to the Badd Company but once he did he
decided that he really liked the lot of them,
even the dwarf.

"I'm sorry I missed your succession
ceremony." Martin said as he walked over to
his wife.

"You had already left the church when I
found out and I was going to send Rydol to go
get you when I received Mozart's note. I
suppose I could have waited until next week
but we might've needed more powerful spells
before that so that's why I did it today." She
explained.

"Well it's a good thing that you did. We
may be going home pretty soon. Maybe you
should try your higher spells on the Shadow
Lord when we go back into the secret room."
The priest stood next to her as she looked out
at the night sky.

"I'm afraid, Martin." Vandrossa admitted.

"It's OK to be afraid my love." He put
his hands on her shoulders.

"You don't understand Martin It's not the
creatures that I fear but facing my people
after what I did with that deep elf." She
shuddered at the thought.

"That was not your doing my love. You
were enchanted by a very powerful wizard and
by The Bright One I will find out who is
responsible and make them pay." He turned his
wife to face him and they embraced one
another.

"I love you Martin." The queen nuzzled
his chest.

"I love you too." He lifted her chin and kissed her passionately but suddenly stopped and looked up.

"Don't let me stop you, please continue." Mozart smiled broadly.

"This is not what it looks like." Martin started but was cut off.

"Of course not, you just continue where you left off and pretend that I was never here." The conjurer slipped back inside before Martin had a chance to explain things.

"Now what?" He looked at his wife.

"Now we tell them the truth when we get back to the war room." She smiled and he relaxed for he was happy to finally be able to tell his friends everything.

The whole company decided to rest for the night and to try again early in the morning. Vandrossa and Martin intended on speaking with them at once but they got distracted as soon as they got to the war room. Hours were spent on trying different things and they started to get ridiculous when Mozart suggested that it might have an allergy to something. They tried silver (again), gold, wood, and bronze but none of those things did anything to it. They started to get creative and even silly but when Falbar threw a cube of butter at it they all stopped. Shazaron and Captain Woolfe came into the room a little later on with lunch in their arms. While they ate she looked at the shadow in the magic circle and cocked her head to the side in thought. She pulled the war hammer from her belt and flung it at the beast just to see what would happen. The creature howled in pain as the war hammer returned to the cat woman's hand.

"What did you do?" Mozart asked as no one else had seen her hit the creature.

"I just threw my hammer at it." She told him.

"Do it again." The conjurer said and she complied. The beast howled again and looked at the cat woman menacingly.

"You hurt it. How is that possible? What kind of hammer is that?" The elf questioned.

"It's a hammer of Odin. Why?" She asked.

"Martin, try your mace." Mozart glanced at the priest who pulled out the holy white mace at his belt and hit the Shadow Lord. The beast again howled in pain and he dropped to one knee.

"These weapons were blessed by deities. It is no small wonder that they would harm such creatures." Martin told his friend.

"Yes but perhaps the weapon need not be blessed by a deity. Try blessing my axe Martin and we'll see if that works." Mozart suggested.

The priest quickly chanted his spell and a brilliant white light engulfed the weapon. The conjurer stepped into the magic ring and hit the unliving beast but did not harm the creature at all. Distraught, he left the circle and tried to think of something else.

"Well it was worth a try." He shrugged as he sat down on one of the wooden chairs.

"Perhaps Martin is not quite powerful enough. Let me try." Vandrossa stated as she conjured the same spell and blessed her elven sword.

She entered the circle trembling with fear and the creature leered at her so she slashed her weapon at it. The beast screamed as its arm came flying off of its body and the room erupted in cheers. They had finally found the creature's weakness and all of their hard work was paying off.

"I suppose I had better put its arm back on before we put it back inside the book." Martin said as he entered the circle.

"Why?" Clint asked but soon burst into laughter as the creature died from the healing spell that Martin cast upon it.

"Well, we can add healing to that list of what hurts a Shadow Knight." Dee said as he held back laughing at the blushing priest.

"Wait, I thought they were called Shadow Lords?" Rydol wondered.

"Actually, I did some research while you all were sleeping," Falbar explained but Mozart silently coughed. "I mean we did some research. They've been calling themselves Shadow Lords to gain fear and influence but they are in fact a powerful group of pseudo-undead created by a lich."

"Pseudo my tubb!" Clint berated.

Falbar just rolled his eyes and continued "OK, now that we've determined what hurts these things we need to plan out our strategy on ridding them from Shaldra's house."

"But first she needs to tell the rest of you where it is she really lives. It's time for you to introduce yourself properly, your majesty." Dee bowed before the elven woman.

"What are you talking about Dee and why are you bowing before Shaldra?" Clint asked.

"My name's not Shaldra, its Vandrossa. Queen Vandrossa Birchbark and it is the capital of Plenty that I ask you to help me free." She stood regally before the company.

"This is a joke right?" Clint asked stunned.

"No, it is not and there is more to this tale. I would like to thank you all for protecting Martin for me for he is my

husband." All eyes fell upon the nobleman and
he stood by her side confirming her words.

"Does this mean that you're not gay?"
Clint asked and was swiftly hit hard in the
arm by Derrkon.

"Oww, what was that for?" He looked down
at the dwarf.

"For disrespecting the King of Plenty."
Derrkon stated and it finally hit the company.

All the assassins that went after the
half-elf and the secrecy behind him weren't
just because of his family but because he was
indeed the King of Plenty. The two of them
explained that Martin posed some kind of a
threat to someone but they weren't sure who.
So long as Vandrossa was single there would be
no heir to the throne but when she married
that would soon be no more. Someone wanted the
kingdom and they were willing to kill Martin
for it. For some reason the Queen was safe by
herself so his identity was kept secret for
both their sakes. A few people were allowed to
know this secret such as Dee who was told
because of special circumstances and Derrkon
who had attended the wedding. Shazaron also
found out somehow and promised to help the
Queen however she could. Now the truth was out
and it was up to each individual person to
decide for themselves if they were going to
help them free the capital city of the elves.

Chapter 4
"Nobody Wants to Stay Behind"

"That's not fair! First you guys get to stay at the palace for two days and now you're telling us that we can't go with you." Mitch complained.

"I'm sorry but that's the way things are." Dee explained as he was filling his travel pack.

"I understand Eric staying because he's only sixteen but not me." He said.

"You're only seventeen." Eric interjected.

"I'll be eighteen in Father's Reflection." His brother reminded him.

"Look the two of you can make any arguments that you want but you are not going and that's final." The nobleman was getting irritated.

"That's OK Eric we'll get Avery to come with us and follow them later." Mitch told his brother after they left Dee's room.

"You'll do no such thing!" Dee shouted after them.

"How are you going to stop us?" Mitch asked.

"Well there are a number of things that I could do but I think the easiest would be to have Mozart turn you into frogs and have my mom take care of you." The nobleman threatened as he joined them in the hall.

"You would not, would you?" Eric looked slightly worried.

"I will if I feel I have to." He looked at the two sternly.

"If it wasn't for us you and the others would have been sold as slaves. I thought we were part of the company now." Mitch said.

"I know but this isn't like taking out slave traders or bandits. We're going to war and we may not come back besides I need you two here to keep an eye on things." Dee tried to reassure the two boys.

"That's babysitters work." The elder brother huffed.

"No I mean it Mitch. With Sket's constant plots to get us killed I fear he may use our absence to his advantage. I want you to stay at Falbar's place to protect his family while Eric stays here to watch our house." Dee had a look of concern on his face.

"Do you really think that the High Magus would bother?" Mitch wondered.

"I think he would try anything to get back at us." The nobleman responded.

"Alright, I'll do it but if nothing happens then I'm going to raise hells the next time you try to make me stay home." He shot Dee an angry look.

"Deal." Synbadd held out his hand and Mitch shook it.

"Why does he get to stay at the fun place?" Eric whined and the two of them just laughed.

It was early the next morning when the company woke up and gathered at Dee's house. They all agreed to go to Clinton knowing that they may never come back alive but they were brothers in arms and they would risk it all for each other. Todd pulled out a traveling pack then looked around at the company curiously.

"Where's my horse? Do you wish for me to run alongside you my lord?" He asked Dee.

"You're not coming." He stated flatly.

"Why not?" The man wondered.

"Because this is not your fight and I could use the extra protection at home." The nobleman explained.

"Begging your lordship's pardon but I don't think you need any protection here especially if you're not going to be present." Todd pointed out.

"Good point. You can come along but only if you call me Dee." He surrendered.

"Thank-you sir." He bowed slightly then ran into the stable.

"Take the brown horse!" The nobleman called out to the man.

"You know if he's going with us he'll definitely need a better weapon then the one he has." Clint pointed out.

"I know. We'll grab him one in Stallarn." He replied.

Todd came out of the stable with the brown horse and the company headed for the south gate. When they got there they were surprised to see Captain Woolfe and a large yet familiar looking tiger woman. It appeared like they were ready to go on a long trip and they were about to leave.

"Are you going somewhere Captain Woolfe?" Dee asked as they met.

"Yes." She answered.

"Really… where?" He wondered.

"With you silly. Oh and it's just Marta while we're traveling." She smiled broadly.

"Since when?" The nobleman inquired.

"Since I ordered her to." The tiger woman answered for her.

"And who might you be?" Dee thought he knew her from somewhere but he just couldn't put his finger on it.

"You know me quite well sexy." She whispered into his ear.

"Shaz…" His mouth was quickly covered with her tail.

"The name's Ronny darling," The disguised archduchess stated as she ruffled the nobleman's hair.

"Very well 'RONNY' but I don't think this is a good idea." Synbadd glared at her.

"Too bad," Shazaron stated flatly.

"Come on then, the longer we tarry here the more of the day we waste." The nobleman grumbled.

"Did you know that there is a wolf following us?" Marta asked as they passed the south gate.

"What?" Dee asked forcefully.

"Right there" She pointed at a blur that ducked behind a building.

"Is that you Paris?" Synbadd stopped his horse and called out.

The wolf came out from behind the small house with his ears down and his tail tucked underneath him. He whined as he slowly approached the mounted man like he had done something bad. Dee got off his horse and put his hand out so the wolf rubbed his head on it.

"What are you doing out here boy?" Synbadd asked calmly and Paris licked his face in response.

"I think he wants to come with us." Derrkon observed and the wolf barked happily.

"He said yes." Vandrossa informed them.

"You can speak with animals?" Falbar wondered.

"How do you think I know what Ax is saying?" She looked at him quizzically from the back of her black winged lion.

"Well I don't know. I just thought that
it had something to do with the bond that you
share." The minstrel replied.

"I'm sorry boy but you can't come with
me; maybe next time?" Dee scratched the wolf's
ears before mounting his horse once more.

They traveled on for a few feet and Paris
continued to follow them so Dee shouted, "Go
home Paris!" The wolf snorted and continued to
travel alongside the company.

"I said go home!" The nobleman shouted as
he waved his hand at him and Paris jumped back
but he wouldn't retreat.

"Shaldra can you please make him
understand that he can't come with me right
now?" Dee asked in earnest.

"I don't believe that he will be swayed
Dee." She informed him.

"It appears that we have picked up yet
another ally." Martin put his hand on the
nobleman's shoulder.

"Fine, I don't care." Dee threw his hands
into the air then pointed at the wolf as he
told him, "You'd better keep up with us and
don't complain the first time you get hit by
an arrow or something."

Paris yelped in happiness as he ran
alongside the nobleman's horse and wagged his
tail as he looked up at him.

"I can't seem to get anyone to stay home
these days." He shook his head in defeat.

"Oh but won't it be more fun to have
everyone here?" Shazaron smiled at Dee.

"Fun? You mean trouble." Synbadd
corrected.

"It's kind of interesting how those two
things always seem to coincide wouldn't you
say?" She urged her horse to go faster.

"Interesting isn't the word I would use."
He mumbled to himself as he signaled his
companions to quicken the pace.

The day was hot but a cool breeze kept
the company from being too uncomfortable on
the road. They traveled at a fast pace but not
so fast that they would exhaust their horses.
The road was relatively quiet which was
unusual for this time of year but the company
didn't seem to notice. No one bothered them
all day, much to the disappointment of Clint
who discontentedly found a suitable campsite.
It was quite a distance from the road and
slightly hidden so that they could see it but
someone traveling on it wouldn't see them.
Mozart started to cast a spell to create a
magical shelter when Dee stopped him.

"What's the matter?" The conjurer
wondered.

"We shouldn't use magic unnecessarily
from now on. It might attract the wrong kind
of attention especially in Plenty." Synbadd
explained.

"Very well, I shall sleep the old
fashioned way." He said as he sat down on a
nearby log and closed his eyes to enter into
the elven dream state which is a different
form of meditation. It is not true sleep but
elves require less rest then most races so
they use this dream state to rejuvenate their
energy. Since they are not truly asleep any
kind of noise can break them out of this
meditation.

Clint built a small fire in the center of
the campsite to warm the area as it was
rapidly becoming very cold. Rydol helped
Vandrossa pitch a small tent as she seemed to
be extremely tired and then joined Mozart in
the dream state. Dee, Clint, Todd, Shazaron,

and Marta unrolled their sleeping bags by the
fire. Captain Woolfe made sure that her bed
roll was the closest to Dee's and she watched
him as he pet Paris and imagined that it was
her. Derrkon put up his tent and joined the
company around the fire. They watched Falbar
struggle with his tent and Clint laughed until
Dee went over to help him. Martin was putting
up his tent until a playful cat woman kicked
the sticks and made it fall.

"What was that for?" The nobleman looked
at her confused.

"You should sleep over there." Shazaron
pointed at Vandrossa's tent.

"Just because everyone here knows who we
are doesn't mean that we should not keep up
the disguise." He told her as he began to fix
his tent.

"You know that could be part of the
disguise. A young handsome priest courting a
beautiful elf maid. I'd believe it." She lay
down on her tummy to watch the half-elf and
just as he finished his task she used her tail
to tear down the tent again.

"I know that you're trying to be helpful
Ronny but it is still too dangerous for the
both of us." He picked up the end of the tent
to try again but Shazaron put her hand on his
to stop him.

"Martin, it may be a long time before you
get to see her again." She looked at him
seriously.

"What do you mean?" he wondered.

"You are not going home to stay. Even if
we succeed you will still need to return to
Haven's Run and keep your identity a secret.
If we fail then these days will have surely
been our last. Do you wish to spend them apart

from the one you love?" Shazaron asked solemnly.

Martin looked down at the wreck that was his tent and thought about the cat-woman's words for a short time. It had not occurred to him that he would have to leave his wife for a second time. He looked at Vandrossa's tent and feared that he might not see her for a long while if at all should they fail. His heart became full of sadness and longing so he dropped his tent and entered into hers. Shazaron smiled at the priest and silently rolled up his tent to put it away.

"Martin… what?" Vandrossa started as he knelt down and pulled her into his embrace.

"Is something bothering you my love?" She asked after a while.

"Please let me stay with you as long as I can. These may be our last days and I want to spend them with you. I want to hold you in my arms and feel your breath upon my body." He squeezed her desperately.

"I want those things as well but what if we are discovered?" The Queen looked into his eyes.

"We are Martin Tierleaf and Shaldra Oaktree. What is wrong with us being two courting elves of Plenty?" He placed a warm hand on her cheek.

"Nothing I suppose." Vandrossa looked down.

"I will do whatever you wish my love but I strongly desire to be by your side while I still can." Martin brought her hand to his lips and kissed it gently.

"Then stay with me." She kissed him as she pulled him down with her and they made sweet passionate love to each other.

Dee set up watches for the night but it wasn't necessary as no one bothered them at all. The next morning they continued on the road and only stopped once to help a merchant fix a broken wheel on his wagon. It was a couple hours after midday when they finally reached the great city of Stallarn. On the outside it looks like a small hamlet but when you ride up to it a wall seems to appear out of nowhere. Once you pass the great gates, a massive metropolis with floating islands become visible all of a sudden. The magical city can be disorientating at times because you can appear at any place you happen to think of at the time.

"So where are we going Ronny?" Dee looked at the cat-woman.

"I have made arrangements for us to stay at The Born Adventurer." She answered.

"Alright, I hope Gloria is working tonight." Clint said excitedly.

"Do you actually have a steady girlfriend?" Falbar asked sarcastically.

"Hells no! I just have a favorite girl in every town I visit." He answered.

"You probably have to pay each of them as well." The minstrel grumbled.

"Only if she's had a rough month but if business has been good then I keep my coin." The soldier elated.

"That's disgusting." He cringed.

"As if you've never paid for sex." Clint stated cruelly.

"Only the one time and I assure you I had no idea that they were harlots." Falbar defended himself.

"Yeah sure, like we believe that story." The soldier loved to see the minstrel squirm.

"Alright, everyone stay here. I have
something that I have to take care of and I
don't want to look for anyone when I'm
finished." Dee announced as they dismounted
and housed the horses, one Dwardelve pony, one
winged lion, and a wolf in The Born
Adventurer's stable.

"I've already booked a boat if that's
what you're going to do." Shazaron informed
the Commander.

"I figured as much Ronny. No there's
something else I need to take care of but it
shouldn't take me long so if I'm gone longer
then an hour send someone to come look for
me." Dee told the company.

"Would you like for me to come with you
now?" Todd asked.

"No thanks my friend. Enjoy yourself in
the tavern." He reassured the man that he
would be alright.

The company walked into the familiar
tavern and only Todd reacted to the massive
stuffed dragon's head in the entry hall. They
all sat at a large table that happened to be
empty at the time and ordered something to
eat. Everyone was happy to be able to sit and
relax for a while before they went on the
river voyage in the morning.

"What is a garn swirl?" Todd wondered as
he looked down the extensive list of drinks
that were served in the tavern.

"You do not want one of those." Falbar
warned.

"Why not?" He asked.

"Last time Falbar ordered one we all got
sick from it." Mozart wrinkled his nose at the
memory.

"Really?" The man looked at them curiously for why would a tavern serve a drink that would make people sick.

"Yeah, apparently only garns can properly appreciate the beverage." The conjurer informed him.

Several drinks later and not quite an hour Dee showed up at the tavern carrying a long wooden box and a crate. He sat down at the table and presented the parcels to Todd who looked at them curiously.

"What are these?" He asked.

"Something you're going to need on our journey." The nobleman answered.

"Can I get you something sir?" A female Broll asked as Todd proceeded to open the crate.

"Bridges' Ale." He answered shortly.

"You know Dee you order that so often it's a wonder you don't try the Flaming Milton." She bumped him playfully.

"Guild Master Grizclaw. What are you doing serving drinks?" Dee looked up at the extremely tall brown grizzly bear woman.

"Actually I'm not taking orders. I was just kidding. I'm here to drop off your boat passes but I see that you have one extra passenger and one wolf." She placed several pieces of parchment on the table.

"Yeah well they were kind of a surprise." He replied.

"Don't worry I'll have that taken care of by morning. I really meant it about the Flaming Milton. It's made with Bridges Ale as well as a few other things. You might like it." She nodded and then left the company in peace.

"My lord," he stopped himself as he looked at the Commander and started again, "I

mean Dee I am undeserving of such raiment."
Todd pulled out a fine suit of chain mail and
a finely crafted short sword.

"Consider it payment for the book." He
waved at him and the man said nothing more.

"Well good night all." Clint said as he
escorted a beautiful blonde girl upstairs.

"Yeah I think I'll turn in tonight too."
Dee said as he left the table. Captain Woolfe
followed him upstairs and tapped him on the
shoulder.

"Is there something I can do for you
Marta?" He looked up at her.

"I'm tired of us just exchanging longing
glances." She bent down and kissed him
passionately.

His only response was to put one hand
behind her back and the other one caressed her
breast. She picked the man up and took him to
her room where they spent the night together.
For the company this was the last night that
they would spend in comfort for quite a while
and they wanted to enjoy every second of it.

Chapter 5
"Winged Attack"

The next morning the company went downstairs to the tavern reluctantly for they weren't quite ready to continue on their way. The last one to arrive was Clint and he was not alone as a young lady was wrapped around his arm. He bid the woman goodbye with a light kiss on her cheek then he put a tan trench coat on and straightened it as he joined the party at the table. The boarding passes that Guild Master Grizclaw promised Dee were waiting for him at the bar but she was not. The nobleman got a letter from the Broll apologizing for not giving them to him personally but she had urgent business to take care of elsewhere. The company ate in silence and traveled to the docks with all of their mounts. They had a bit of trouble with Vandrossa's black winged lion for he became extremely nervous boarding the boat. In the end she had to put him to sleep and then levitate him into the cargo hold.

A squat human man with one eye, one leg, and a white beard greeted the party warmly and introduced himself as the ship's captain. He wore a strange black suit with gold trim and held a smooth black onyx pipe in his hands. At his side was a cutlass with strange writing on it which Mozart believed was fairy script but he wasn't quite sure. They each had their own individual rooms below deck which they were shown to right away. After the ship left the dock they all got an invitation to the captain's cabin for dinner. Most of the day the company either stayed in their quarters below deck or wandered aimlessly around the ship. Later on when the two suns hadn't quite set all of the way the party gathered together in the captain's cabin where a long dinning table had been set for them.

"Where's Shaldra?" Dee wondered as they all sat down.

"Ah, yes where be that fine young elf maid?" The captain asked in a scratchy voice that foretold of the many years that he had smoked.

"I wish to apologize for her absence on her behalf Captain Barbosa but she is not feeling well. I believe she's a little sea sick. I've done what I can to alleviate her condition but it still persists." Martin bowed slightly.

"Oh well that sometimes happens but very rarely with an elf though, they usually love the water you know." He responded.

"Yes, that is kind of odd considering that she lived on a boat for quite a few years when she worked with my uncle." Dee commented.

"She worked with your uncle?" Martin wondered.

"Yeah, he talked about her quite often when I trained with him. He says he misses the days when she was there on the barge. Didn't you know that Martin?" The nobleman looked at him curiously.

"Um, well we haven't had much time to talk about her past much considering that she's well over five hundred years old" He looked down as he blushed.

"I understand." Dee smiled reassuringly.

"I'm always amazed to hear the age of an elf. Especially one as beautiful and young looking as your companion." Captain Barbosa stated as he buttered a piece of bread.

"If it's any comfort to you Captain even us elves cannot tell how old anyone of our kind is. I didn't know Shaldra had lived so long." Mozart enlightened.

"Lord Bridges something outside approaches." Rydol informed him as he put his hand on the hilt of his sword and headed for the door.

"What is it?" He asked as he got up to follow the elf.

"I don't know but it sounds like a hundred pairs of wings." The soldier replied.

Suddenly there were screams coming from the sailors on deck and the running of feet could be heard echoing throughout the ship. The Badd Company ran outside only to see a horrible sight of small winged creatures attacking the men on deck. The beasts had strange bat-like wings that stretched out three feet and they had fat insectoid bodies. The most frightening feature they had was the long needle-like proboscis that ended with a small spear. The creatures were using the spear to penetrate the skin of their victims and sucked their blood dry making their corpses look like prunes.

"Needle Bats! Don't let them get attached to you!" Rydol warned as he drew forth his elven sword and cut one in half in mid-air.

Dee pulled out his two swords and joined the elf in swatting the flying terrors out of the sky. Clint rolled out of the way as one of the creatures dived bombed him and he sliced its wing off causing it the hit the deck in a bloody mass. Martin on the other hand was trying to help the sailors that had the beasts attached to them. He quickly discovered that it was a bad idea to pull the proboscis out without immediately using magic to seal the wound for he nearly killed a sailor as he began to bleed profusely. Mozart and Falbar

started to cast their spells and fire burst
out in several directions killing many of the
flying beasts. Derrkon joined Martin in his
quest to rescue the sailors that were being
sucked dry by the nasty little creatures. Todd
took up a position behind Dee and cut the head
off a needle bat that nearly plowed into his
commander.

"Thanks." Bridges nodded as he cut apart
two more.

"My pleasure Synbadd," Todd responded as
he batted away another one.

Shazaron and Marta looked like they were
performing some kind of dance as they spun
about slaying needle bats left and right. The
cat-woman with her war hammer and long knife
and the wolf-woman with her cutlass in hand
quickly became surrounded in a pile of dead
carcasses. Just then Clint got struck in the
leg and left shoulder blade by two of the
beasts. He dropped to one knee as he elbowed
the one on his leg knocking it out but he had
a hard time reaching the one on his shoulder.
The soldier's strength was waning fast and he
had to do something before he lost
consciousness. He decided that a body slam
would do the trick but found that to be folly
for even though he killed the monster its
proboscis penetrated deeper into his body.
Clint got up off of the deck and silently
walked over to the priest lazily killing a few
needle bats as they got too close to him.

"Martin, I do believe that I'm going to
need your help." The soldier said as he fell
forward unconscious before the half-elf.

"Clint!" He shouted as he saw the needle
bats attached to him.

One of the beasts was still alive as it
started to move and continue to suck out the

soldier's blood. Martin pulled out his white
holy mace and smashed the beast apart before
it regained its full strength. He pulled out
the one on the soldier's leg and healed it
immediately but was shocked when he looked at
the creature that Clint smashed with his body.
The proboscis had gone completely through his
shoulder and the priest wasn't sure if he
could pull it out on his own.

"Derrkon, I need your help!" Martin
shouted desperately.

"Let me guess you need me to pull
something out of someone. By Bargovin's forge,
Clint! I might not be able to pull this one
out and even if I do he may die from blood
loss." The dwarf explained.

"I know I need help taking him below deck
to Shaldra. She'll be able to help us with
this." He picked up Clint's feet as Derrkon
grabbed his shoulders and the two of them went
down stairs.

It seemed like a hopeless battle as the
warriors kept killing needle bats but they
just kept coming. It didn't look like they
were making any headway at all and they were
starting to tire. Mozart was beginning to
think that something was not quite right with
this swarm of beasts when Falbar got hit in
the stomach.

"Are you OK Fal?" The conjurer asked as
he created a fire shield and prevented three
of the creatures from reaching the two of
them.

"Does this look alright to you?!" He
responded as he turned around and pointed at
the thing in his stomach as he screamed in
pain.

"Stand still." Mozart pulled out his
battle axe and prepared to swing.

"Are you trying to cut me in half?!" The
minstrel panicked.

"No just the needle bat." The elf swung
his weapon and the back half of the creature
fell on the deck.

"Oh, that's just lovely." Falbar stated
as he fainted.

Mozart bent down to help his friend and
when he went to pull the creature's proboscis
out of the minstrel he was stopped by Rydol.

"What is it?" The conjurer asked.

"If you do that without healing him right
away then he will die from blood loss in less
then one minute." The elf explained.

"So what do we do?" Mozart asked.

"Wait for one of the healers to help him
out and watch our backs." Rydol said as he
sliced three bats in one swing of his Elven
blade.

"Won't he die anyway if he is neglected?"
Mozart asked as he started casting another
fire spell.

"No, their needle nose is designed to
create a hole in the skin in such a way that
the blood can only enter into the tube under
the spearhead. Oww!" The elf cried out as a
winged beast cut in front of him and opened a
long gash down his cheek.

"You know an awful lot about these
things." Mozart said after his fire spell
engulfed ten of them in a large fireball that
exploded high above everyone's heads.

"I once commanded a platoon of soldiers
when we got attacked by these foul creatures.
I lost two men before we figured out not to
pull the needle out of their bodies without a
healer present. I also know that your friend
will be alright for awhile as it took us three
days to travel to the nearest healer and three

of those men had a needle bat attached to them." Rydol explained as he continued to kill the monsters.

"Do they normally travel in a swarm like this?" The conjurer wondered.

"Not as far as I know of." He answered.

"I thought not." Mozart said as he started to conjure once more.

Dee and Todd were still back to back and they had several dead bodies littered on the deck before them. They had several cuts on their bodies where the needle bats clawed them but thankfully there were none attached to them. Their strength was draining fast and Dee looked over at the disguised cat woman to see that she and her friend were suffering from the same problem. The Commander signaled to Todd that they needed to join with Shazaron and Marta to strengthen their position. It was slow going but they finally reached the Ani-women and they created a small protective circle.

"We can't keep this up forever." Dee said as his swords started to feel heavy in his burning arms.

"No, but it's fight or die!" Woolfe shouted.

The four just kept batting away at the flying terrors as they flew in a circle around them. Their weapons and armor were soaked in the rancid blood and guts of their foul enemies. Just then a bloated needle bat hit Dee's right arm and his short sword went flying as he was too weak to keep hold of it. The weapon went soaring through the air over the side of the boat and was seen no more. After that Todd got hit in the arm and the beast firmly attached itself to him and Shazaron got one on the back of her neck.

"This may be the end." Marta said as two of them hit her in the back.

"Maybe, but I'm not willing to give up just yet." Dee swung at several more creatures but he completely missed.

"If we're to come to an end then I'm glad you are here with me." The wolf woman grabbed his hand and held it tightly.

"Me too." He smiled weakly at her just before two beasts hit him square in the chest and he fell backwards.

The situation did indeed look to be hopeless as the company slowly dropped one by one from exhaustion. Just then a bright light surged outward and engulfed the entire ship. Everyone that was still left alive had to cover their eyes to keep from being blinded and when the light finally dimmed away they received quite a shock. Every last one of the flying terrors left the area and scattered away like scared sheep. It took a few minutes for the group to recover from the shock but finally Shazaron broke the silence.

"What happened?" She asked.

"Ask Mozart." Rydol responded.

"It took a little while but once I realized that the creatures were being controlled I conjured a spell to disenchant them." He explained as he bent down to check on Falbar who was starting to regain consciousness.

"What happened? Did we win?" The minstrel asked as he looked up at the mage.

"In a manner of speaking… yes, but not without costs." He pointed at the man's belly.

"Oh, I see." He looked at the front half of the needle bat that was still attached to him and fainted once more.

"Where's Martin and Derrkon. We need their healing powers." Rydol wondered.

"We are here." The dwarf answered and they all looked to see him and Martin helping a rather sick looking Vandrossa up the stairs to the ship's upper deck.

"You look positively dreadful Shaldra. What's the matter?" Shazaron asked as her and Woolfe brought the injured over to them.

"Sea sick," She stated flatly as the dwarf and her husband gently helped her sit on a large pile of ropes.

"Interesting" The cat woman said as she lifted Falbar off of the floor and brought him over to the three healers.

They sat there and healed their company before turning to help the injured sailors on the deck. It didn't take long as the sailors that were well helped them bring the injured over to them. They were also lining up their fellow sailors that were dead on one side of the deck while tossing the needle bats over the side of the boat. Dee looked down the long line of dead men and then turned to Vandrossa.

"Can you bring them back to life?" He asked her.

"Well..." She was cut short.

"There'll be none of that on this ship. My men will be given a proper burial at sea as they rightly deserve." Captain Barbosa interrupted, "Or in this case, the river!"

"I'm not powerful enough to bring back the dead when their bodies are in that kind of state anyway. If they were slain by normal injuries I could but since they were drained of all their blood and their bodies are like shriveled prunes I cannot. Nor would they want to come back in the condition that they would

be in." The elf explained with a grim
expression.

"So Mozart you said that these things
were being controlled?" Shazaron called and
got everyone's attention.

"Yes, by a very powerful wizard but I
can't tell who it was, fore they were blocking
me from seeing them." He answered.

"Were they near by?" Dee asked.

"They had to be at least when the swarm
was first summoned but after it arrived they
probably teleported away." The conjurer
explained.

"So they could have been a passenger on
this ship. Captain Barbosa, if it's not too
much trouble I would like to see the ship's
manifest to see if any of the passengers
slipped away while we were fighting." Synbadd
looked at the man seriously.

"Of course Lord Bridges, I'll get that
for you right away." The man gave a curt bow
before disappearing below deck.

"You know Dee it could have been someone
disguised as a crew member as well." Mozart
pointed out.

"I know I was going to make sure that
they were all accounted for as well. Where's
Clint?" He asked as he noticed that the man
was absent.

"He's fine but he needed to rest for a
little while. His injuries were quite
extensive and it took quite a bit of magic to
save his life." Vandrossa explained.

Clint groaned as he woke up in a not so
comfortable bed. It took him a few minutes to
realize where he was and what had happened. It
appeared that the Queen of Plenty had once
again saved his life. At this rate he would

never be able to repay her even though she wouldn't ask him to he still felt obliged. He looked around the small room he was in and noticed that he was half naked. The man smiled at the thought that the elven woman always seemed to find a reason to take off his clothes but then shook his head violently as he remembered that she was married to Martin.

"That's too bad but I guess he really does deserve her." He said to the empty room as he sat up.

He still felt a little weary but he wasn't about to let that fact stop him. He wanted to know if everything was alright and if the little monsters were taken care of, fore if they weren't he wanted another taste of them. As he began to dress himself he soon realized that all must be well for he no longer heard the sound of battle up above and he knew that people were still alive for a few sailors casually walked past the room. The soldier finished getting dressed then looked at his prize trench coat and gave a slight groan as he saw the fist sized hole in the shoulder. The spot was covered in blood and bug guts so he tried to clean it off in the wash basin that was in the room. Fortunately the bug guts came off quite easily but not the blood stain. Disappointed, he hung the coat over his arm and went to search for his companions. It didn't take long to find them as they were nearby in the captain's cabin discussing the events that took place that night.

"Well all of the passengers and the crew are accounted for so the spellcaster couldn't have been one of them." Dee stated after Clint sat down on a chair at the table.

"That just means that whoever it was either was on board invisibly or they scried the boat, teleported on board, summoned the swarm, and then teleported away. Either way they are no longer with us." Mozart explained.

"How do you know that?" Clint asked.

"Shaldra cast a spell to detect enemies and Martin Divinated but neither of them found anything." Dee informed the man.

"So what do we do now?" Derrkon wondered.

"For now we can do nothing more but be extremely cautious. Hopefully the rest of our trip to Tarsk will be undisturbed. In the meantime, we should all get some rest but I want one of us on deck at all times to keep a look out just in case." The Commander ordered.

"I'll take the first watch. I don't think I could get any rest right now if I wanted to." Mozart volunteered.

"Good." Dee patted the elf's shoulder as the company filed out of the cabin.

"What's the matter Clint?" The conjurer asked the soldier who looked a little down trodden.

"Those little jerks poked a hole in my favorite jacket and the stain won't come out." He held the trench coat up for the elf to see.

"Well I could easily take care of that for you." Mozart smiled as he held out his hand to receive the object.

"Really? OK but only fix the hole I want to keep the stain." The soldier handed the jacket to him.

"Why?" The mage wondered.

"So it will give me a constant reminder to give the man that caused it a similar stain on his clothing." Clint had an evil looking smile on his face and the elf understood his

friend as he repaired the damaged coat with
magic.

Chapter 6
"The Home Front"

Eric hated the fact that he and his brother were left behind like they were still children. He knew that he wasn't quite a man yet but the company accepted the two of them as equals or so he thought. It didn't make it any easier when his brother got to stay at Four Star Falbar's while he grudgingly stayed at home. He understood that Dee just wanted to protect them and it wasn't as if he didn't appreciate everything that the nobleman did for his family. He just wished that they wouldn't treat him like he was still a boy and recognize that he was now a man.

Eric was sitting in the lounge brooding when he heard a loud crash come from the kitchen followed by a scream. It was Lady E and quicker then anyone could possibly accomplish the soldier was rushing through the door long sword in hand. He stopped suddenly when he saw two grubby looking men holding Dee's mother with a rusty knife to her throat.

"'Ere now put the sword down lad or the lady tastes m'blade." The man ordered Eric and he complied.

"Tha's a good boy now kick it 'ere." He nodded.

Eric wasn't sure what to do but he did know that even if he complied they were planning to take Dee's mother with them. That wasn't something that he was about to allow and a sudden inspiration hit him. He placed his foot under his sword and made like he was going to kick it over to the dirty little man but instead his flipped it into the air hurling it at the man's head. The blade flew past Lady Enid Bridges and hit its mark right it the middle of the fiend's forehead. The other man stood in shock as Eric quickly freed his weapon and slew the assailant before he knew what hit him.

"Oh Eric!" Lady Bridges wrapped her arms around the soldier and started to cry.

"It's OK Lady E, I'm here." He reassured her.

Just then the kitchen door flew open and four more men bearing short swords burst into the room from outside. They looked down at their fallen comrades and looked up at Eric with hate filled eyes. The man stood protectively in front of the noblewoman as he tried to lead her to the dining room door.

"Don't take another step boy." The tallest of the men said with a raspy voice.

"You mean like this?" He side stepped once more and Lady Bridges stayed behind him.

"Oy 'e jus' took another step Rog." One of the other men pointed at Eric.

"Oh that's nothing." The soldier smiled as he took two more steps with his foster mother close behind.

"Shut your trap Horis and you… I told you to stop." This man was obviously the leader of the bunch and stupid was written all over his forehead Eric thought.

"And who's going to make me?" He asked as he took a few more steps.

"Fred, kill him!" The leader of the thugs shouted.

A gangly youth stepped forward with his sword in hand and gave Eric an evil looking toothless smile. His weapon flashed and the soldier blocked it with ease but this boy was almost as fast as he was as his blade narrowly missed Eric's face.

"Run Lady E!" The soldier shouted as he lunged forward forcing all of the trespassers to step back.

The noblewoman ran for the door leading deeper into the safety of her house while Eric did his best to keep the ruffians at bay. The soldier's blade was a blur of parries and blocks as all four men ganged up on him. The young scout watched as Enid retreated and as she did so he smiled broadly at the attacking men.

"Now you're in it deep." Eric's teeth flashed as he broke one of the dirty swords in half.

"I think you're the one tha's in trouble boy." One of the men said.

"Yeah, you're out numbered four to one." Another man pointed out.

"You poor simple fools, I was taking it easy on you for the lady's sake but now that she's safe I can deal with you properly." Eric cut across one man's chest while stabbing another in the gut.

"Why you insolent little maggot!" The leader lunged forward and the soldier was barely able to move out of the way but not before he cut a large gash along his left arm.

"You cut 'em Rog." One man elated to his folly as Eric plunged his weapon deep into the man's chest.

Four men lay dead on the kitchen floor while the other two stared blankly at the soldier. He side stepped and prepared for another attack when they heard another crash come from somewhere behind them. The thug leader smiled broadly as he stared at the man before him.

"That ought to be my men right about now." He gloated.

The kitchen door swung open as Eric jumped to one side and prepared to defend himself from both sides. Much to the soldier's delight and much to the thug leader's dismay it was not more reinforcements. As a matter of fact four men wearing the red tunics of the Haven's Run guard stepped into the kitchen bearing arms. The thug leader having seen no way out of it dropped his weapon and surrendered. The soldiers immediately arrested the two men and clapped them in irons.

"Scout McAllister, are you alright?" One of the men asked.

"I'm good." He answered.

"Eric!" Lady Bridges ran up to him and hugged him fiercely.

"I'm fine Lady E." He smiled at her.

"But your arm!" She exclaimed.

"Just a scratch, nothing a gnomish healer can't handle," He reassured her.

"Then you'd better get over to one right away." She told him.

"But what about…?" The soldier was cut short.

"I said now! These other soldiers can handle this mess." Lady Bridges ordered and he silently obeyed.

Eric fully intended to do as the noblewoman asked but then his thoughts suddenly turned towards his brother. What if this was not just a random attack on the Bridges home? Dee did ask him and his brother to stay behind to protect both the nobleman's family as well as Falbar's. As he ran down the street towards Four Stars he bound his wound, then he suddenly remembered that his brother said something about visiting some girl's house today. He immediately turned down another street just in time to see his brother kissing a brown haired girl goodbye.

"Hey Eric, how's it going?" Mitch greeted.

"Fine I guess. How was your visit with Cara?" He wondered.

"Well let's just say that I'm no longer the boy I once was and have stepped into manhood." He answered.

"No way! With Cara? How was it?" Eric asked stunned.

"That my dear brother you will have to find out on your own." He put his arm around his brother's shoulders and leaned on him slightly.

"Wait till Clint finds out. He'll announce it to the whole world." The soldier was absent-mindedly leading them to Four Star Falbar's.

"You don't have to tell him you know." Mitch stopped him in the road.

"I wasn't going to but you know that he'll find out about it through one of Cara's friends. Those girls can't stop gossiping for nothing." He looked at his brother.

"You're right." Mitch snorted then blurted out. "Eric your arm!"

"Huh? Oh yeah I forgot about that. I came looking for you because Dee's house was…" His voice was drowned out as the two brothers heard a large bang echo down the street.

They ran towards the commotion only to stop dead in their tracks at the horrific scene before them. Four Star Falbar's was on fire and many people were running through the streets screaming. Numerous soldiers were heading for the fire when several small green creatures poured out of the famous tavern. They had squat little bodies, bald heads, and long pointed ears. Two of them carried a woman while three more carried a man and they headed for the south gate.

"David! Wanda!" Mitch shouted and the two men drew forth their weapons to attack.

A group of the Haven's Run guard joined the fight as the two brothers clashed weapons with the goblins. Mitch's long sword and battle axe slew many beasts as he tried to reach Falbar's parents while Eric's long sword cut him a path. The soldiers weren't making much headway as the goblins neared the south gate.

Suddenly, one of the soldiers burst into flames and three more fell from the small creature's weapons.

"Eric, take out their spellcaster!" Mitch shouted as he killed two more.

The soldier ran towards the goblin that was spouting strange words and swung his weapon at him only to hit nothing. The goblin finished his spell and vanished right before his very eyes. Eric looked around to see if he could find where the little creature went when he felt a sharp pain in his back. He turned around and saw the spellcasting goblin grinning with a bloody dagger in its hands. The soldier put his hand behind his back and felt hot blood dripping down his finger tips. The goblin again started spouting strange words but this time Eric would not let him finish as he took what was left of his strength to slice the beast apart before falling into nothingness.

Mitch on the other hand was drawing nearer and nearer to the creatures that held his friend's parents. Many of the little green goblins panicked and turned to run but not the largest of the bunch. He shouted in their crude language and three stopped running as they formed a defensive line between the bounty hunter and Falbar's parents.

"If you're thinking of stopping me tochee then think again." Mitch said as he fell one of the beasts in the line.

The big one said something incomprehensible and the three remaining goblins rushed the man. He stepped to the side as the first two went by and parried all but one sword swipe from the big one. The cut along the side of his leg stung but Mitch endured as he stabbed one of the little ones in the gut. The other one squealed and ran in fear but the big one just stabbed the fleeing goblin in the side killing him for his insubordination. Now it was down to the big goblin and the bounty hunter. The two of them circled each other as they sized one another up trying to judge their next action. The goblin moved first and sorely missed as Mitch's axe batted his weapon aside. The man then brought down his other weapon and cut the head off of the beast.

"Well, that was disappointing." He looked down at the dead creature then continued to pursue the other fleeing goblins.

Many of them got past the guards at the gates but not the ones carrying Mr. and Mrs. Teroth. Mitch was glad that he was able to catch up to them before the beasts got away with kidnapping them. His weapons were nothing but a blur as he frantically slew goblins left and right. He gave Dee his word that he wouldn't let anything happen to Falbar's parents while they were away and he wasn't about to break that oath now.

"Hey, you men up there!" he called to the guards atop the battlements. "What are you gawking at? Drop the portcullis. Don't let these beasts get outside the city!" Mitch shouted at the soldiers on the battlements but it soon became clear that they were in some kind of magical trance.

Realizing that he would never make it to David and Wanda in time to save them by going through the little monsters he started to run around them. If he couldn't kill them all before they left then he would prevent them from leaving as he ran up to the battlements. He pushed passed the dazed soldiers and quickly released the counter weight that held the portcullis aloft. The iron bars fell down killing five goblins and preventing the others from escaping. Proud of his achievement, he jumped down among the remaining goblins and the ones carrying Falbar's parents dropped them as they drew forth daggers. They quickly surrounded the bounty hunter and together they rushed him. With one great swing of his sword he blocked all but one of their attacks. This time a dagger stuck out of his back leg and he started to lose his strength. The creatures were about to rush the man once more when several Haven's Run guards arrived and started to cut them apart from behind. It took mere seconds for the soldiers to slay or capture the remainder of the foul beasts.

"Thanks a lot guys." Mitch smiled weakly.

"No it is us that should be thanking you bounty hunter." One of the men spoke.

"I'll take you up on that offer as soon as I find my brother." He replied.

"Scout McAllister has been taken to the Healer's Huts." He informed the man.

"Well then I think that I as well as the Teroths need to be taken there at once." He stated as he fell to one knee.

    The soldier helped him up and slowly led
him and the Teroths to the Healer's Huts on
the other side of the city. Mr. and Mrs.
Teroth were thankfully unharmed as they were
just knocked out. Eric's wound wasn't that
deep but if it wasn't for the quick action of
the guard he might have bled to death and
Mitch suffered only minor wounds. When the
four of them were fully recovered they went to
survey the damage done back at the tavern. It
wasn't as bad as they had thought for the
townsfolk were quick enough to form a bucket
brigade to put the fire out.
    "Well, it's not that bad." Wanda Teroth
said as she looked inside.
    "I suppose this gives us an excuse to
finally remodel the place." David shrugged.
    "Yeah, you could build a bigger stage for
Falbar." Eric piped in.
    "Clint would really love that idea
wouldn't he?" Mitch joked.
    "I can see it all now. Clint telling us
that Falbar's head has gotten as big as this
stage." And the two brothers laughed.
    "Thank you boys, if it hadn't been for
you who knows were we'd be now." Mr. Teroth
stated.
    "Actually it's Dee that you should thank.
He's the one that told us to stay behind and
keep an eye on things here." Eric informed
him.
    "Speaking of which we had better check on
Dee's house just in case they attacked them as
well," Mitch said as he headed for the door.
    "Actually they did but I took care of
that lot. Lord Clay has probably got a few
soldiers guarding the place right now." He
told his brother.

"You know, I'm never going to hear the end of it." The bounty hunter sounded glum as they traveled down the street.

"Hear the end of what?" His brother asked.

"How Dee was right by making us stay behind." He answered.

"Oh that. Somehow I don't think that he'll say I told you so although Clint might but who pays attention to him." Eric tried to cheer his brother up a bit.

The two men laughed as they got home and sure enough there were ten extra guards at the Bridges' home. They didn't know who attacked them exactly but they knew what they were after. The McAllister brothers also knew that they had better keep a constant vigil for more trouble as Dee's worries were confirmed. They feared for their friends lives now for if they had this kind of trouble at home what kind of dangers were the others facing and would they come home alive?

Chapter 7
"Trouble on the Way"

The company had reached the elven city of Tarsk without further incident on the river. The city was uncommonly quiet for being a port town and trade hub but the company thought that it might have something to do with the Shadow Knights. They bid the captain of the ship farewell and went to re-supply their travel packs at the general store.

"Clint and Derrkon come with me while the rest of you get what we need to continue." Dee ordered as they stood outside the shop.

"Where are you going?" Falbar wondered.

"To the blacksmith; I need to purchase a new sword." He answered.

"What happened to the old one?" Clint asked.

"Lost it overboard" The Commander grimaced from the memory.

"The magical one you got from Stallarn?" The minstrel gasped.

"Unfortunately yes," He answered through gritted teeth.

"I'm sorry for your loss." Vandrossa looked at him.

"Don't worry about it Shaldra. It wasn't that much of a loss, besides it won't do much good where we're going anyway." Synbadd smiled and the three men left the company in search of a blacksmith.

The rest of the party watched them for a second before entering into the general store. It was a little different from any of the general stores that most of them had visited before although most of the elves knew what to expect. The store had wide open aisles and everything was neatly organized unlike most general stores where there was barely room for one person to go down an aisle at a time. There were also a few things that could be found here but in no other store like barrels of fresh picked berries and bins of strange looking leaves. The company also noticed the lack of things such as dried meat and animal pelts.

"Wow I've never been in an elven general store before. I had no idea that they were so different." Falbar said as they wandered about.

"Yes, I find it to be most comforting. No offence Falbar but human general stores always smell like tobacco and dead animals." Vandrossa said as she grabbed a handful of dried fruit and put it in a bag.

"None taken, Shaldra." He smiled as he examined a strange wooden carving sitting on top of a glass case.

"Welcome, friends. Can I be of service?" A five foot tall thin male elf with long black hair greeted them with a musical kind of voice.

"Yes, we require a few things." Mozart handed the man a piece of parchment with a list of supplies on it.

"Very well sir. Kayfax come here." He called and an elf that looked to be about ten years old (in truth he was about fifty) came running from the back of the store.

"Yes father?" The boy looked at the store keeper.

"Gather these things for our good patrons and be quick about it." The elf ordered his son.

"Yes sir!" The boy took the list and immediately went about his task.

"Not many elves from Hytarr come through
here. Where are you headed if you don't mind
my asking?" He asked Mozart.

"Um well we're…" The conjurer wasn't sure
what to tell the man.

"Going to Clinton to celebrate the
Festival of Life." Vandrossa filled in for
him.

"Ah, yes nowhere is the celebration more
sacred or more beautiful than in…" The elf
stopped suddenly then gasped in surprise as he
looked at Vandrossa.

"Your majesty!" He exclaimed as he bowed
low before the Queen.

"Good sir I do believe that you are
mistaken in my identity." She tried to
convince the elf but he wasn't buying it.

"No my lady, I would know you anywhere
for I once served in the royal stables as a
young man." He stayed on the floor at her
feet.

"What do we do now?" Falbar wondered.

"Rise" The Queen said in a commanding
voice.

"Yes, your majesty." The elf slowly got
to his feet and then Vandrossa grabbed him
forcefully and stared directly into his eyes.

"I am not the Queen of Plenty. I am a
simple passerby." She stated in a strange
hypnotic voice.

"Just a simple passerby," the elf
repeated entranced.

"Martin, get the boy." She looked at her
husband.

"Please don't hurt me! I promise not to
say anything!" The boy shouted in panic.

"I mean you no harm Kayfax." Martin spoke
in a soothing voice.

"What are you going to do with me?" He asked as he calmed down slightly.

"Just make you forget what you heard." Vandrossa looked into the boy's eyes and he also stared at her hypnotically.

"Forget what I heard." The boy repeated in a strange tone.

"What did you do to them?" Woolfe asked.

"I charmed them though I hated to do it but we really have no choice. We can't afford to have rumors flying around that I'm not in the capital city right now." The Queen explained.

"I wasn't expecting anyone in Tarsk to recognize you. I apologize your majesty for my mistake." Rydol bowed before her.

"There is no need for that Rydol. I should have been prepared for this." She put her hand on his shoulder.

"So what do we do now? You obviously can't wander around looking like that now can you?" Falbar inquired.

"I've always wanted to be a blonde." She smiled brightly as she looked at her husband and he blushed slightly.

"Well then that should do it sir," The store keeper said as he packed up the last of their things into large leather bags oblivious to what happened earlier.

"Thank you." Mozart grabbed the bags one at a time and handed them off to the others in the party.

"You enjoy that festival now." He called after them as they left the store.

They joined Dee at the blacksmith's as for some reason they weren't ready and the nobleman explained that his horse Snowmane threw a shoe. The blacksmith was just finishing up when they got there.

"Hey guys, who's the babe?" Clint looked at a disguised Vandrossa.

"That's Shaldra stupid." Falbar shot him an angry look.

"You look better as a red head." He said after staring at her for awhile.

"What happened?" Dee whispered to Martin after they were out of earshot of the blacksmith.

"She was recognized," his friend answered.

"We should have expected that." Synbadd frowned.

"Yes I suppose we should have." The half-elf sounded worried.

"What's the matter Martin?" The nobleman asked.

"Many things," He answered solemnly.

"Do you want to talk about it?" Dee was concerned for his friend.

"There is not much that can be done about my fears. Having to sneak into my homeland like a thief only adds to them," The noble priest explained.

"Don't worry my friend. One day you will be able to walk through your homeland without fear and all will know you for who you are." He smiled and somehow it made the half-elf feel better.

The company spent the night in Tarsk without further incident and headed for the capital city the next morning. They discussed going through Wood's Edge but Vandrossa and Martin assured them that it would be safer not to mention faster if they went through the forest instead. Dee was slightly worried about getting lost.

"I've been to Plenty," the Commander began, "It's not easy to traverse the dense woodland without a guide." He and Derrkon exchanged a knowing look but they were both suddenly embarrassed as both Vandrossa and Rydol laughed.

"The day that the Queen of Plenty gets lost in her own kingdom is the day the world turns upside down." She smiled brightly and nothing more was said on the subject.

For the first three days they traveled without incident but as they got nearer to the capital they all felt an ominous presence in the forest. The silence was deafening as there was a lack of forest noises and the company's animals were uneasy. Under normal circumstances they would hear a low musical song resonate through the forest so near the Festival of Life but there was no music.

"The influence of the Shadow Knights has gone far to have the trees feel so full of fear." Vandrossa commented.

"Indeed, when we first entered the forest I felt like it was almost home even if Hytarr is the place of my birth but now." Mozart shuddered from a chill that did not exist.

Suddenly all of the animals except Paris reared up as if defending themselves from an unseen enemy. The wolf growled at something and then leapt into the air landing on nothing as it appeared that he was floating in mid air. Luckily no one was riding their mounts at the time so everyone was able to draw their weapons to fight the invisible assailants.

"Mozart, make these things visible so that we can fight them!" Dee shot out as he saw a fanged bite mark appear on his horse Snowmane.

The company slashed about at nothing while the Hytarr elf conjured his spell and the animals continued to fight the invisible enemies. A spray of glitter shot forth from the elf's finger tips and covered the whole area but nothing new was revealed by the magical dust. Dismayed Mozart began to cast a different spell and a light rain began to fall but again the magic didn't reveal what was attacking the animals.

"Dee, these things are either highly resistant to my spells or they are not invisible at all." The elf informed their commander.

"You are right Mozart it is a forest spirit but why is it attacking us?" Vandrossa wondered.

"You mean that we're being attacked by an undead monster?!" Falbar's voice squeaked slightly.

"No the forest spirit is not undead." Martin stated calmly.

"They're definitely not undead or else Tecklar would've told me!" Clint blurted.

"We should send the animals away since they are the only ones getting attacked." The queen looked at Mozart and the two started to conjure.

All of the animals disappeared except for Vandrossa's winged lion and Dee's wolf. The conjurer started to cast another teleport spell for the two remaining animals when the Queen stopped him.

"What's the matter?" He asked her.

"They do not wish to go." She answered.

"So how do we hurt this forest spirit?" Dee asked as he tried to help Paris.

"Vandrossa, can you speak with it?" Martin looked at her with concern.

"I shall try. Gasa huku xa bas je se vib." She spoke calmly and then bowed slightly.

"Ve ka je quy U keys vak je?" A strange voice answered her.

"Is that Elvish?" Falbar wondered.

"Yes, it is an ancient root language of elvish that is rarely used anymore." Mozart explained.

"Like that spoken by Numina and her people?" Synbadd wondered of him, the Conjurer simply nodded and listened to the conversation being had.

"U yub Vandrossa thas er qua atierhay." The Elven woman spoke to the air.

"What are they saying?" Falbar asked.

"Shaldra announced that we mean the spirit no harm and it wanted to know who she was so she told it." The mage paraphrased to the minstrel. (From this point on I shall write the translation under what was said for those that are interested. The first sentence was 'Peace spirit we mean you no harm' then the spirit replied 'Who are you that I can hear you?' and the queen said 'I am Vandrossa Queen of the elves.')

"Xava quas le je kusim reit kaywikahay we lawke ba?" The spirit asked.

(Why then do you bring foul creatures to destroy me?)

"Xa vena keim se reit kaywikahay." She looked confused.

(We have brought no foul creatures.)

"Qua kahass er aha vik ba." A blue light surrounded the two animals.

(The presence of these hurt me.)

"That is strange." Vandrossa furrowed her brow.

"What?" Dee wanted to know what was going on.

"According to the spirit the presence of Ax and Paris hurts it." She explained.

"How is that possible?" Martin asked.

"I don't know but that would explain why all of the forest animals have abandoned the area." She answered.

"So what do we do about them?" Dee pointed at the wolf and the winged lion.

"Let me ask the spirit. Vex keys xa gee queim quha kay xukew vikus je?" The Queen was worried that they might have to leave her and Dee's companion behind.

(How can we pass through this area without hurting you?)

"U le sew zex," was the reply.

(I do not know.)

"It doesn't know." She looked at Dee.

"Why don't we walk around its territory?" Shazaron asked.

"That will only work if its territory doesn't cover Clinton but I will ask it. Vex ryak hu jehey tysil?" The elf inquired.

(How far is your land?)

"Reb vaka we qua kezas kez," it answered.

(From here to the broken rock)

"I was afraid of that. I know this spirit and its territory spans to cover the entire forest but its roots are strongest around the capital. I'm afraid that Ax and Paris will have to stay behind." She informed the party.

"Teleport them to my house Mozart," Dee ordered the conjurer but again the spell did not work on them.

"OK now what?" The nobleman threw his hands into the air.

"Ax's pride." Vandrossa said.

"What?" Synbadd looked at her confused.

"Ax's pride must be around here somewhere. They wouldn't have wandered too far from the capital. If we can locate them then they can protect our friends until we rid

ourselves of the evil that is affecting the
spirit." She explained.

"How can we do that?" Falbar wondered.

"It's called a locate creature spell
Fal." Mozart looked at him as if to say duh.

"Oh right." The minstrel blushed
slightly.

"You know it's been bothering me as to
why the spirit would all of a sudden get hurt
by the presence of animals. Do you really
think it has something to do with the Shadow
Knights?" Martin wondered.

"He's right. If it's not the Shadow
Knights that have changed the nature of the
forest spirit then destroying them will not
solve the problem. Without animals, the forest
will slowly die and the Plenty elves with it."
Mozart pointed out.

"Martin and I can Divinate together to
find out what we can do to solve the problem."
Vandrossa offered.

"Alright we'll set up camp a bit away
from the area that the spirit started to
attack us and if you two don't come up with
something then we'll try to find Ax's pride.
We really can't spend more then one extra day
out here." Dee started to lead the party the
way they came.

"Quayz je huku rek jehey wetakyssa. Xa
tux le ek paw we kaweka je paykez we sekbite."
Vandrossa bowed before she turned to follow
the nobleman.

(Thank you spirit for your tolerance. We
will do our best to restore you back to
normal)

"U jay quy je le rek U vena sew pas ratus
tax er toywa." The spirit answered her and it
could be heard no more.

      (I pray that you do for I have not been
feeling well of late.)
      "Vandrossa, if we have Derrkon join us we
could form a divine commune and get a stronger
Divination." Martin suggested after they
helped set up camp.
      "If he's willing" She looked at the
dwarf.
      "I would be most honored." He bowed
slightly.
      The three of them walked a short distance
away from the campsite and sat down on their
knees facing each other. They held out their
hands palms facing outward and touched each
other to form a triangle. Martin started the
chant and the others joined in as they all
closed their eyes concentrating on the problem
they wished to solve. Suddenly it was like the
small group was floating in air and traveling
through time and space till they stopped in
the grand tree city of Clinton. It felt so
different to the two elves that had lived
there for so many years but the dwarf noticed
nothing since he had only been there once
before. The city was quiet except for a few
hushed voices and it was cold like death
itself lived there. A grand tree that held the
most beautiful and sacred citadel aloft was
once bright and cheerful but no more. There
was always music playing in the great halls to
bid the elves that were departing to the
heavens in the west goodbye but not now. The
three of them traveled to the center of the
great tree to see a shining light but it
suddenly dimmed and changed colors. Instead of
the bright golden color it was it became a
dark red and a great sadness could be felt
throughout the three divine servants. Then
just as suddenly as their divination started

it ended and they were back in the forest looking blankly at each other.

"Well I hope the two of you understood what was shown to us for I don't see how the city of Clinton is connected with the forest spirit." Derrkon stated.

"What did you see?" Falbar asked as he had been watching the three with fascination ever since they started the divination.

"It wasn't the city that we were shown but the Arden tree." Vandrossa told the dwarf.

"Arden, now that sounds familiar." The minstrel said more to himself than anyone else.

"I believe that the spirit you spoke with belongs to that tree." Martin surmised.

"Yes I've spoken to the Arden tree on many occasions." The Queen stated as they headed back to the campsite.

"I know I've heard the name Arden before and I don't just mean the sacred trees." Falbar closed his eyes as if that would help him to remember.

"So it was the spirit whose light we saw change?" The dwarf asked.

"I believe so." Martin replied.

"Arden, Arden, Arden." The minstrel kept repeating.

"What can be done to help the spirit?" Derrkon ignored the confounded man.

"Song" Vandrossa looked at the two baffled men.

"What do you mean by that?" The dwarf wondered.

"There has always been singing in the halls of the great citadel. The music speaks to the spirit as most are sung in its language and now that it has stopped it has become saddened from loneliness." Vandrossa explained.

"So if we sing in ancient Elvish the spirit will leave our animal companions alone?" Derrkon asked.

"Perhaps, but which song?" Martin inquired.

"One of our most powerful; the song of life," the Queen stated solemnly.

"Aha! That's the name of the elf's heaven!" Falbar elated suddenly.

"Yes, the Arden tree comes from the heavens. There are only three of them on this continent; one in Clinton, one in Clennross, and the last in Glave. These trees were gifts to our ancestors by Falanna and we protect them above all others. Falbar do you have any paper and ink left?" Vandrossa turned to look at the minstrel.

"Of course I do, me without any writing implements is like a day without a night." He pretended offense. "And it was my understanding that there are four trees."

"I apologize I just thought that you might be out since you've been writing so much on this trip." She blushed slightly. "As for the trees we commonly only refer to the three since the fourth was lost."

"That much I know and you need not apologize, I was just feigning offense. I did run out of ink but was able to purchase more in Tarsk. What do you need it for?" He wondered.

"To write a song for you to play for us tomorrow. You are extremely well versed for a human." Vandrossa noted of the minstrel. He blushed slightly as she turned to Mozart. "Do you know the song of life in the ancient tongue?" She asked the conjurer.

"Since I was a child," He answered her.

"Would you mind joining Falbar, Martin, Rydol, and myself tomorrow? The more voices we have the stronger the song." She explained.

"Did you just say me?" Rydol suddenly asked.

"Yes." She looked at him and smiled brightly.

"But I don't sing." He looked away apparently embarrassed.

"You can't fool me Rydol. I've heard you and you have a most enchanting voice." That statement only made the soldier even more embarrassed.

"I would be honored to join you in song." Mozart bowed slightly.

"Hey, how come I wasn't asked? You just sort of volunteered me just like you did Rydol." Falbar teased.

"Well, I suppose I figured that you would love to learn a song in another language and couldn't pass up the opportunity to perform it. Besides you are the only one that carries around an instrument." She looked at him apologetically.

"You're right! When can we get started?" He pulled out several pieces of parchment excitedly.

"Great, now everyone's encouraging him to play that thing." Clint complained.

"Shut up or I'll make you sing along with them." Dee scolded him and everyone laughed.

"Over my dead body," Clint whispered as he crossed his arms over his chest.

Vandrossa started to write the long and elaborate song onto Falbar's paper while Martin and Mozart tried to teach him how to speak the language properly. The minstrel was an apt pupil as he easily learned the lyrics

and the tune that went with it but he didn't
want to stop there. He made Mozart teach him
more of the language until he was too tired to
continue. If nothing else, tomorrow was going
to be an interesting day.

Chapter 8
"The Way In"

The company broke camp and Falbar was all too ready to get started with the elven song that he just learned. He stretched his fingers as he readied his lute and began to play the elven Song of Life. His voice was soft and the elves enjoyed listening to him sing the first stanza before they joined him. It was true what Vandrossa said about Rydol's voice but hers was even more enchanting. Martin brought an innocent gentleness to the music while Mozart's voice was playful and slightly wild. The Song of Life produced a gladness in the hearts of the company and even Clint smiled broadly but when anyone looked at him he quickly turned it into a grimace. They passed the place where the spirit attacked their animals the day before and nothing happened this time. As a matter of fact the company felt like a protective hand had been placed on their shoulder. After a while it felt like the forest was coming alive and everyone soon forgot about their troubles. That is until they saw a massive stone wall surrounding the city and the singing party members stopped to look at them with contempt.

"Those weren't there when last I visited this place." Derrkon pointed out.

"No, the Shadow Knights created the surrounding walls as soon as they captured the council." Vandrossa explained.

"Looks like they closed up the docks as well," Dee observed.

"So how do we get in?" Falbar wondered.

"There is only one gate on the north eastern side of the city." The Queen informed the party.

"We'll just have to have some sort of disguises if we are to enter into the city." Clint stated.

"Actually only Woolfe and I need to go in the front gates while the rest of you wait on this side of the wall." Shazaron spoke with authority.

"I don't think so." Dee looked at the two women.

"Well I suppose that no one here will recognize you sexy but the rest will definitely need to stay out here so that we may make other arrangements for them." The cat woman said playfully.

"What kind of arrangements?" Vandrossa asked nervously remembering what happened the last time she tried to sneak past the guarded gates.

"Hopefully it won't be too scandalous?" Martin said as he held his wife's hand protectively.

"Don't worry Martin it's not scandalous at all but that is a very interesting thought." She smiled devilishly.

"I don't even want to know what you were thinking." The nobleman blushed under the cat woman's gaze.

"Well Dee, shall we go?" Marta grabbed hold of the nobleman's hand.

"Yeah, I think we should." Clint stepped forward.

"No you should stay here." Dee ordered.

"What? No way man! No offence Shazaron but the three of you shouldn't go alone just in case something goes wrong!" The soldier shouted.

"I need you to stay here to safeguard the Queen." Synbadd said with a hushed voice.

"Yeah but…" The man was cut off.

"I'll take Todd with us?" He suddenly decided.

"Me? Are you sure?" Todd asked nervously.

"If anyone could pull us off as bandits, it's you." Dee placed his hand on the man's shoulder.

"I suppose so." He looked down in shame and embarrassment.

"Don't worry about that. I told you I have a way in for us but we all can't go at once." Shazaron stated confidently.

"Of course your grace," Todd bowed low and then backed away.

"Oh no you can't back out of this now cutie pie you're coming with us." The cat woman put her arms around Todd and his ears turned slightly pink.

"Humph I guess the newbie's your new sword buddy." Clint crossed his arms across his chest as he sat down with his back against a tree.

"Why Clint I didn't think you cared enough to get jealous." Dee teased.

"I'm not jealous! I just wanted to go right now. I'm sick of all this waiting all of the time." The soldier looked away angrily.

"Don't worry my friend as soon as we all get into the city there will be plenty for you to do." Synbadd rubbed the top of the man's head and he just waved him off.

With a shrug and a wave the four of them headed towards the north eastern side of the wall leaving the others to wait for them. As they neared the city gates Shazaron pulled out four black cloaks and handed them to the rest of the party. They grabbed them and Dee just looked at it strangely as Todd and Marta donned the garment.

"What's this?" Synbadd wondered.

"Don't tell Martin but these are robes of Mistarra, goddess of darkness."

"I know who she is," Dee almost growled in memory of his last dealings with the goddess in question and they were right here in Plenty.

"I figured that he couldn't handle coming in through the gate this way. I suppose some of the others could have come this way as well but why complicate things. My people are prepared to retrieve them one at a time if we have to." Shazaron explained.

"Your people?" The nobleman looked at her curiously as he grudgingly pulled the robes over his head.

"You didn't think I came here alone did you?" She smiled broadly.

"What are you talking about?" He stared at her intently.

"You'll see." She flicked her tail and then led the way ahead.

Dee's question hung over his head as he silently followed Shazaron to the front gates. It was heavily fortified as many soldiers guarded the gates but they had no markings indicating who it was they served. They were stopped but when Shazaron glared at them like they had done something wrong and they let them pass without further investigation. When they went by the gates they were faced with a horror that they were not prepared for. The once beautiful and sacred city of the elves was a dismal pile of dirt as the people were forced to dig up their homeland. Many lines of chained elves were covered in dirt and blood as they dug large holes in the ground.

"Maybe it would be best to leave Shaldra and Martin outside. To see this would be devastating." Shazaron whispered to Dee.

"No they would want to avenge this injustice and restore their land to its proper state." The nobleman replied.

"Yes I suppose they would. Come this way." The cat woman ordered.

She led them to a church that had apparently been dedicated to Mistarra but looks can be deceiving. Shazaron greeted a tall grey wolf man with a strange kind of hand shake and he silently led them to a door. Behind the door was a holy (or unholy as any good divine servant would call it) font dedicated to the goddess of darkness. The wolf man pressed on the holy symbol which was a black star set inside a black hollow circle and the font moved to the side revealing a dark passageway. The wolf man then pulled out a small glowing gem and led the four of them down the secret hall. The stone doorway closed behind them with an ominous thud as they continued onward. At the end of the hall the wolf man pulled out a strange object that looked like a cat's head with a white lightning bolt on the forehead and placed it in a niche on the wall. An archway magically appeared and the wolf man held out his hand as if to indicate that they should go first. Shazaron led the way and after everyone passed him the wolf man pulled the token out of the wall just as he too entered the room beyond.

"I take it Shazaron sent you?" The wolf man said after a time.

"Greydon it's me." She smiled at him.

"Your grace?" He cocked his head to one side and then the cat woman dropped her disguise.

"Shazaron!" A small five foot tall black cat man with bright green eyes came out of

nowhere and pounced on her as several others
appeared as well.

"Valtarr when did you get here?" She
asked as she kissed his forehead.

"About a week ago. I know you told me to
stay home but I couldn't let you go on a grand
adventure without me." He smiled and rubbed
his head on her hand.

"So you mind telling us what's going on?"
Dee interrupted the happy reunion.

"Sorry, allow me to introduce Greydon and
Valtarr from Clan Dameron. This is Synbadd and
his companion Todd from Haven's Run." She
introduced them.

"OK so your friends are your mystic clan.
What are they doing here?" He wondered.

"I've been having them filter into
Clinton a few at a time. The Shadow Knights
believe that they are servants of Mistarra and
it's a good cover as most of the soldiers fear
us almost as much as the Shadow Knights." The
cat woman explained.

"Great so how do we get everyone else
inside the city." Dee asked.

"That's easy. Everyday hunters leave the
city and return with fresh meat for the
church. We simply replace them with our people
and they can come back the same way that we
did." Shazaron told him.

"Won't it be suspicious to have that many
new servants of Mistarra appear in one day?"
The nobleman wondered.

"No, since we've been bringing in several
clan members everyday no one will even
question them but if they are questioned then
they know what to do." She said.

"One of us should go with your hunting
party so that Clint won't hurt any of them

before everyone else realizes that they're on our side." Synbadd suggested.

"Marta will go back. There are so many black wolf men in the city right now that they won't even notice." She informed the nobleman.

"How are they going to replace the hunting party? I don't know if Mozart will be able to morph everyone or not." He questioned.

"Do you think Clan Dameron is nothing but Ani-men? Besides the Shadow Knights have placed magical devices on the outside of the gates that would unmorph them. I made sure that someone was sent that looked similar to everyone in your group. Everyone that is except Todd here who was a surprise but we figured out that problem on our own didn't we?" She rubbed the top of Todd's head and Valtarr looked away suddenly but only Dee seemed to notice.

"Greydon go ahead and send the hunters out. Oh make sure they have an extra cage large enough to store a wolf and bring extra rope for the Queen's lion. You'll need to bind his wings down so he won't hurt himself." Shazaron ordered.

"Yes my lady." The grey wolf man bowed and left the way he came with Woolfe following him.

"Now shall we go into the war room where I can show you the plan?" The cat woman looked at Dee.

"Lead the way my liege." He nodded his head and the two men followed her deeper into the hidden lair.

They entered into a large room where several cat men, two wolf men, three humans, and two elves stood. A white tiger man greeted the archduchess and then showed her the map on the table. They had placed red dots where

Shadow Knights were known to hang out and green dots where the council was kept. Dee looked over the map and discussed tactics with the tiger man who was introduced as Shadeclaw. Shazaron on the other hand slipped out of the room to speak to Valtarr about his disobedience.

"I can take care of myself." He told her after she lectured him for awhile.

"This is not a game Valtarr. You could get hurt or even killed." Shazaron said.

"So could you." He shot back.

"Yes but unlike you my training has been completed for quite some time while you are not yet a full member of the clan." She had a touch of worry in her voice.

"I am a man and I can make my own decisions as to what I'm going to do." The cat man whispered.

"I realize that you are a man Valtarr but I am the clan leader and I will be the one to tell you when you are ready. That is why I'm ordering you to stay here while the battle goes on tomorrow." Shazaron spoke sternly.

"But…" He started to protest but was stopped.

"But nothing, you're staying here and that's final." She glared at Valtarr and nothing more was said on the subject.

The company waited patiently for some word from Dee but several hours went by without any sign of his return. They were starting to get worried that their commander got caught or worse. Clint was angry as he kicked a rock into the air and hit Falbar square in the chest.

"Oww, what did you do that for?" The minstrel rubbed his chest.

"Oops sorry," He said but somehow Falbar didn't believe that it was an accident.

"How much longer do we have to wait before I can tear apart those undead fiends?" A voice from Clint's belt complained.

"I know what you mean Tecklar. We should forgo this sneaking around crap and storm the gates." The soldier looked at his sword.

"That would not be wise." Someone on the side of him stated.

"Whoa Woolfe! Where'd you come from?" He jumped slightly much to the minstrel's delight as he had seen her approaching.

"You weren't keeping very good watch if you did not see me coming." She answered him.

"Ha, ha she told you." Falbar laughed but quickly stopped as the soldier glared menacingly at him.

"So what's the plan?" Vandrossa asked.

"You will need to put these on and disguise yourselves as huntsmen." The wolf woman pulled out a bunch of furs and placed them on a pile so everyone could get them.

"What about Stalfax and Paris?" The Queen wondered.

"Stalfax is not here." The minstrel stated.

"Yes he is." She looked at him strangely.

"Where?" He demanded.

"Right here" She put her hand on the massive winged lion's head.

"I thought his name was Ax." Falbar looked puzzled.

"That was just his traveling name just in case someone might recognize Stalfax as the name of the Queen of Plenty's mount." She explained.

"Oh, wait until Stalfax hears about this." The minstrel smiled.

"Who?" Now it was her turn to look puzzled.

"Just an elf we know." He answered.

"Oh, well it is a common Elven name. It means valley people." The elf informed him.

"Really?" Falbar was curious and wanted to ask more questions but was interrupted.

"Enough of this talk! Let's get out of here already." Clint demanded impatiently.

"We must wait until the others return." Woolfe told him.

"What others?" Falbar wondered.

"The ones whose place we will be taking when they return with their hunt." She answered.

The plan was simple, they were to go in as the hunters that left and they would in turn go inside the city later as followers of Mistarra. The wolf was put inside a cage as was the winged lion after much fuss about binding his wings. As they reached the gate entrance the company seemed to become extremely nervous especially Vandrossa but thankfully nothing went wrong. Everyone was shocked to see the city in the state that it was in and the elves being treated so badly but there wasn't anything that they could do at the moment. The King and Queen both recoiled when they saw that they were entering an evil temple but Woolfe assured them that it wasn't as it seemed. It didn't take them long to join the rest of the team in the hidden war room and the Queen quickly joined in on the planning of the assault. She pointed out a few mistakes that anyone would have made except for someone who knew the city as well as she did. It was the first time any of them saw her take charge and the first time they truly understood that she was the Queen of an entire nation.

"We only have two problems and that's getting into the council chambers before the Shadow Knights start killing nobles and making sure that everyone has a blessed weapon." Synbadd announced.

"Actually we only have one problem. Our small group can enter through the secret passage located here." Vandrossa pointed at the heart of the tree.

"What secret passage? We've been all through that area and haven't found anything." Greydon inquired.

"That's because only the royal family can use it. As for the second problem, if we can liberate the High Patriarch then we won't have any trouble making sure everyone's weapons are blessed." The Queen informed the group.

"Well that's going to be quite difficult considering he's one of the guys being guarded." The wolf man stated.

"Is he being held in the same place as the councilors?" She asked.

"No, I think he's in the dungeon." He answered.

"Do you know which cell?" Vandrossa wondered.

"This one" He pointed on the map.

"It has to be a set up." She stated.

"What do you mean?" Dee asked.

"That cell has a secret passage that leads over here to the guard room." She drew a line with her finger.

"Why is it there?" Falbar wondered.

"It's used to place undercover guards in the prison when we need information out of a prisoner." She told him.

"Well that's brilliant." He said.

"Thank you I had it installed when I became Queen but it wasn't my idea. I got it from Tiberius." She looked at Dee.

"How many people know about it?" Greydon asked.

"Everyone in the guard and I'm sure that the Shadow Knights could have extracted that information from someone." The elf answered.

"Then you are probably right in thinking that it's a trap." The wolf man looked down.

"So where else could they hold the High Patriarch?" Shazaron asked.

"I'm not sure but… wait did you just say High Patriarch?" He looked at the cat woman.

"Yeah, I thought we made it clear as to who we were talking about." She answered.

"Then I do not believe that they hold him for they are calling that prisoner a High Matriarch." He explained.

"That's interesting, why would they make that mistake?" Falbar wondered.

"Perhaps because we are a female dominated society they assumed that a woman would be head of the church but not all political positions are filled with women as is evident by the members of the council. This may be a good sign then. Where have they been keeping the priests?" Vandrossa looked to the wolf man.

"They are mining like the rest of the city folk." He answered.

"Can we get to them so I can point him out?" She wondered.

"Yes, you can disguise yourself as a water bearer. After you find him we will be able to replace him with one of our people and no one would be the wiser." Greydon told her.

"Good then let's do it." She ordered.

It didn't take long for them to find the High Patriarch and he almost blew the Queen's cover when he saw her. Fortunately the guard took his elation as gratitude for the water the Queen offered and he was able to get free of his bonds. They replaced him with an elf from Clan Dameron and it was as everyone suspected as no one was the wiser. These small victories encouraged the band of infiltrators and hopes were high as they prepared for the siege that was to take place tomorrow.

Chapter 9
"The Siege"

It was an hour before dawn and dew started to form on the Queen's elegant elven sword as she crouched down before a great oak tree. Vandrossa was covered in a long green cloak that hid her features well and she was tense as she thought of the upcoming battle that was to begin soon. She and Drava, the High Patriarch, spent all night blessing the many weapons of Clan Dameron so that they may hurt the corrupted beasts calling themselves the Shadow Lords. She was frightened not for herself but for her people fore if they did not succeed in overthrowing their captors then everyone would surely be slain and the capital city of the Plenty elves would fall. She was overlooking the large holes that the Shadow Knights forced her people to dig when she felt a warm hand on her shoulder.

"You don't have to go." It was Dee, the Commander of the Badd Company.

"What?" Vandrossa was half in a daze.

"You and Martin can stay here while we overthrow the Shadow Knights." He was offering her a way out but she would not take it.

"No, I need to go. Besides you can't open the secret gateway without me." She told him.

"We could find another way in." He suggested.

"Thank you Dee for your concern but we need all the help we can get. Anyway we're as good as dead if this doesn't work out. I would rather die fighting for the freedom of my people then to die a coward hiding behind my supporters." She stood up and went inside the hidden door in the oak tree.

Synbadd held a great respect for the Queen before but now he had a whole new outlook on her. She was not like any ruler he had ever heard of. She was willing to do everything for her people and never once thought of herself. She was kind, brave, and believed that she was in the service of her people not the other way around. No wonder his friend Martin fell in love with her, he probably would have too if she wasn't already taken.

"It's time Dee, everyone's ready." Clint pulled the Commander out of his thoughts and into the secret passageway.

The plan was to hit the Shadow Knights in as many different places as they could and in the confusion free the councilors. Shadeclaw was to take ten mystics and assault the outer walls, Greydon was to take out the whip masters at the pits, and Shazaron was to attack the outer walls of the palace with Woolfe while the Badd Company snuck in through the secret gateway to free the council. It was a good plan and hopefully it would succeed but the hard part would be fighting the Shadow Knights, especially when anyone killed by them would become a Shadow Knight themselves.

Vandrossa led the company through a series of underground tunnels to a stone circle with Elven runes carved around it. She indicated that the party should stand in the center of it while they waited for the signal. It seemed like an eternity passed while they waited even though only ten minutes went by when they heard the large explosion coming from somewhere above. Vandrossa quickly chanted the ancient words that opened the portal and the company found themselves in a small hall of the palace.

The Shadow Knights screeched their displeasure as they saw the company open the side door into the council chamber and they immediately attacked. Clint led the charge as his sword would not allow him to do otherwise and the two of them were a blur of fury and pent up tension that was finally released. Synbadd and Todd were at each others side with a wolf at their feet when they took down their first Shadow Lord. The wolf yelped playfully when Dee congratulated him for biting the corrupted beast's arm while he was able to cut him apart. Paris and Stalfax were blessed by the queen before the battle, even though she wasn't sure if that would work but it made the animals happy. Martin barely dodged a swing from the jagged sword of a Shadow Knight and hit it with his holy mace blasting it into oblivion. Falbar was struggling with one of the creatures when another one hit him from behind. The minstrel got up despite the pain he felt in his back and slashed his broad sword at the two Shadow Knights forcing them away. Derrkon helped his friend by slicing one of the recoiling beasts in two with his battle axe while Mozart who really wanted to use his spells barely blocked the attacks on him. Rydol stood before his Queen and wouldn't allow any of the corrupted unliving near her while she shot several blessed arrows into many of them. Her lion stood next to the elven captain clawing and biting one until it disappeared in a puff of black smoke. The battle was going well for the company and just like everyone hoped the Shadow Knights were more concerned for the party than they were for the members of the council.

Outside the battle was not going well as Shadeclaw and his mystics were starting to

falter. They were expecting only twenty guards
at the gate as there was usually only that
many there but they were met by twice as many.
The tiger man took out four men before he
realized how outnumbered his troops were and
when half of his mystics were slain he tried
to call for a retreat but there was nowhere to
go. He rallied what was left of his friends
and they created a protective circle that
served them well. They were able to kill all
but ten of the soldiers before a Shadow Knight
appeared to aid in the defense of the front
gate. Shadeclaw's katanas cut apart two men as
one of his mystics fell at his side and the
Shadow Knight cut off the arm of another. The
tiger man became enraged as he and his friends
fell four more soldiers as well as wounded the
corrupted monster but it was still alive. The
soldiers in turn killed the one armed man as
well as two others just as Shadeclaw's weapons
pierced the hearts of two men. The Shadow
Knight seeing the tiger man as the bigger
threat turned to face him as the other mystic
killed one more soldier. It seemed hopeless as
the unliving beast cut across the tiger man's
chest several times but he still stood his
ground. The soldier and the last mystic killed
each other as the battle between the tiger man
and the Shadow Knight raged on. Shadeclaw
roared in anger and the ground seemed to shake
with fury but this didn't bother the shadowy
figure as it took the opportunity to slash
apart his right arm. The tiger man fell to his
knees and he held out his arm to stop the
ground from hitting him. The creature hissed
in victory as it raised its sword for the
final blow and its eyes glowed red with
pleasure. Shadeclaw blocked the attack and
with the strength he had left he plunged a

dagger deep into his own heart. The tiger man would rather die by his own blade then to live as one of those foul abominations for all eternity. The Shadow Knight bellowed in fury as the tiger man fell before him with one last effort he turned to face the creature to show his toothy grin and then Shadeclaw was no more.

Greydon was doing a lot better against the whip masters than he thought as the elven slaves rose up to help them. The wolf man thought that all of the fight had been taken from them as they were forced to tear apart their land. He soon found out that they were just waiting for the right opportunity to take it back and no one was going to stop them. The elves were able to take out the soldiers easily enough but when six Shadow Knights showed up they became helpless. That's when Greydon and his men were needed as they had the only weapons that could hurt the unliving monsters. Two Shadow Knights fell before one of his men died and instantly became dark-touched and one of them. Furious the wolf man picked up the blade of his clansman turned evil and plunged it deep where his heart should have been. None of his men would live as one of those creatures if he had anything to say about it. After that he tossed the blade to a willing and obviously capable elf as he quickly slew the nearest Shadow Knight to him. The three remaining creatures were easily overpowered and killed but before they could celebrate their victory four more Shadow Knights appeared with a contingent of forty soldiers. Greydon growled as he leapt at the nearest shadowy creature and sliced off its head but before he landed he cut across the back of another causing it to disappear as well. The two remaining Shadow Knights slashed at him at the same time. He was able to block one attack but not the other as the blade opened up the side of his body. The wolf man ignored the searing pain as he lashed out at the one that cut him to no avail. He was losing strength and fast but he was not alone as three mystics quickly surrounded him protectively. They would not allow their master to fall into shadow if they could help it and in their fury they slew the remaining unliving monsters. The extra soldiers proved to be no match for the elves who had been saving their wrath for this very moment. Greydon was taken to the freed priests and his wound was seen to. They healed him as best as they could but a patch of black fur that contrasted his dull grey fur grew over the wound and would stay with him for the rest of his life.

Shazaron and Woolfe's group easily took out the Shadow Knights guarding the outer gates to the palace. She stood atop the battlements and sent the flare signaling their success in taking back the gates. Another flare was shot up from the pits but when none came from the outer wall the cat woman frowned.

"What is it?" Woolfe asked her.

"Shadeclaw's group is either still fighting or has failed." Shazaron looked down at her friend.

"What should we do?" The wolf woman wondered.

"You take ten men and find out what's happened and help Shadeclaw if he needs it. I will continue into the palace with the rest to help out Dee." She told her.

"These men can take care of it on their
own I should go with you." The captain
protested.

"No Marta they will need you especially
if there are still Shadow Knights left. I will
be fine on my own besides, soon I will be
joined by Dee and his group." The cat woman
smiled as she bounded down the stairs of the
battlements and into the courtyard.

A little disgruntled the wolf woman
complied as she took ten mystics with her to
the front gates. Shazaron on the other hand
took the remaining twenty and headed for the
council chambers where she was to meet with
the Badd Company. As they traveled through the
halls they ran into several Shadow Knights but
never more then two or three and they were
easily dealt with so they were surprised when
they got to the main doors to the council
chambers. Twenty Shadow Knights loomed
protectively before them and ten more came out
of nowhere behind them. This was far more then
they expected and it felt like they had just
set off a deadly trap. Shazaron knew that they
couldn't surrender and that she needed to kill
as many of these beasts as she could before
they got any of her men. She couldn't expect
help from Dee as she knew not what was going
on inside or even if they were still there as
the two groups glared at each other. The cat
woman suddenly roared as she leapt up into the
air and landed before the twenty unliving
beasts before her hammer first. A loud
thunderclap resonated from the weapon forcing
the Shadow Knights back as the mystics
attacked the ones behind them making an
opening should they need to retreat. Shazaron
killed four of the ones in front of her before
they got a chance to recover from the shock

wave created by her holy weapon. The battle soon became rough as many Shadow Knights were slain only to be replaced by fallen mystics. Soon both sides were down to ten but that changed as two mystics became Shadow Knights. Shazaron had no choice but to retreat as two more joined the ranks of the corrupted creatures. The cat woman threw her long knives at one of them as she ran while the rest of her team threw shurikens. Two Shadow Knights that were once comrades dissipated as the mystics were able to easily out distance their foes. However they now started to use spells against the group as two more of the evil monsters fell into nothingness. A ball of lightning hit all of the remaining mystics as well as Shazaron but she was protected by her weapon. Not wanting any more of her people to become an undead shadow she ran by herself into the line of Shadow Knights slaying two as she went by. She turned in one smooth movement to use this tactic one more time but when she killed the two she ran by one of them hit her in the leg causing her to slide and fall hard on the floor. The six remaining Shadow Knights loomed above her and one raised its weapon to strike her but a black blur flew passed just as the sword came down. The weapon missed the cat woman and instead hit someone else. Shazaron was shocked to see her friend Valtarr lying on the floor bleeding. He had leapt in the way of the blade that was about to hit Shazaron for he would not see her become one of those creatures.

"Valtarr!" The cat woman shouted as she scurried on all fours to reach him.

"Hello, Shazaron fancy meeting you here." He looked up at her and smiled.

"Idiot, I told you to stay out of the way." She pulled him into her lap as the Shadow Knights closed in on them.

"I couldn't let you have all the fun." He placed a hand on her cheek as he breathed heavily.

"Valtarr, don't leave me!" Shazaron cried as tears poured down her face.

"Run, my love. For I can feel my life drain out of my body and I would hate to be the one that causes any harm to you." He kissed the palm of her hand and the Shadow Knights raised their weapons in unison.

"No more shadows will be created in my realm!" The Shadow Knights turned in the direction of the voice and recoiled at the bright light before them.

Synbadd's group entered the room swiftly. Vandrossa had managed to recover a powerful object from the city vault that would aid in the utter destruction of all the Shadow Knights in the city. In her hands she held a tiny pearl in the shape of a teardrop. Legend has it that the pearl was formed when the great Vina Birchbark, mother of the line of Plenty queens as well as deep elves, cried at the stump of the great Arden tree of Lochewood. When her first tear fell upon the wood this pearl was created from it. Its power comes from her grief at her daughter's betrayal who cut the tree down for her own power hungry ambitions. With her will to heal it, Vina, it is said, laid upon the dying tree and died herself. Although her sacrifice was not enough to restore the tree, the pearl was given the power of great healing abilities but only for her children and her children's children. Vandrossa closed her eyes and spoke the words that would invoke the power of the pearl. A light rain began to fall inside the halls of the palace and everywhere there was a Shadow Knight screams of agony could be heard from them. As they slowly melted away into nothing and everyone that was wounded slowly started to heal until they were fully revived including Valtarr who did not quite die yet. The Queen was able to save him as well as the other five mystics that were with Shazaron before the lightning ball hit them.

"Great save!" Shazaron shouted happily after helping her friend get up off of the floor.

"Thank you." She smiled brightly.

"What is that anyway?" Mozart wondered.

"We call it Vina's Tear and now I must use it to help the others." She looked at Dee who nodded approvingly at her.

The whole company followed her around to help with the evil soldiers and other things like clean up. All that is except Valtarr who silently slipped away with any luck unnoticed. He was suddenly embarrassed by his confession to the archduchess and he hoped that she forgot all about it but that wasn't to be.

"Where are you going Valtarr?" His heart skipped a beat as he heard Shazaron approach.

"Back to the church," he stated flatly.

"Why?" She asked.

"To await my punishment for disobeying you once more" He looked down at the floor unable to meet her gaze.

Her right hand gently stroked his cheek and he closed his eyes tightly as if to drown out the sensations she was inducing. When he did this she put her left hand on his other cheek and drew him into a passionate kiss. For a few moments they stood together like that and for him time seemed to stand still until he broke the contact by putting his hands on her shoulders and gently pulled away.

"Please stop Shazaron." He breathed heavily as his body shook with desire for her.

"I thought you wanted me." She said as she looked into his green eyes.

"I do with all of my heart but I do not wish to be one of your play things. I cannot be with you because I would want too much and I'm not willing to ask for anything that I am not worthy of. I will wait for my punishment at the church." After that he ran away.

Valtarr left the archduchess alone in the hall to think about his words and for once she was at a loss. What exactly it was he wanted from her she did not know but one thing's for sure she was not about to punish the man that had saved her life. This was something that she would have to think long and hard about but for now she merely ran off to catch up with her friends.

Chapter 10
"The Council Meeting"

There was much rejoicing as the Queen of Plenty marched the healing pearl through the city. Many elves followed the parade and by the end of the day all of the evil that once controlled Clinton was either dead or run off. The chains that held the people captive were broken and the ugly wall that surrounded the city was knocked down. The pits were filled and as the elves started to sing once more and the land itself started to return to its original vigor. Those that were slain by soldiers were restored to life including the great tiger man Shadeclaw. The celebration lasted all night and Clan Dameron was honored as well as the Badd Company. The queen made a stirring speech thanking the heroes for their bravery and apologizing for the fact that this siege was best left unknown to the populace of Plenty at large. Everyone agreed given the past events that the nation had already suffered, adding this would only serve to nurture the insecurity of the elven people. However Archduchess Shazaron would be known to all as an elf friend as it was her people that came to the Queen's aid. Everyone enjoyed themselves at the grand party and they were invited to stay through the Festival of Life which lasts a whole week. After Shazaron accepted the Queen's offer she went to Marta for help as the cat woman was still confused by Valtarr's words.

"So he finally confessed his feelings to you." The wolf woman stated.

"You knew?" The Archduchess cocked her head to one side curiously.

"Of course I did. It was all too obvious, at least to everyone sitting on the sidelines." She quickly added as the cat woman furrowed her brow.

"Why didn't you tell me?" The cat woman wondered.

"Somehow I didn't think that would help either one of you." She answered.

"What do you mean? Aren't we friends? I thought we shared everything together." Shazaron asked.

"We do but I'm also Valtarr's friend and he didn't want you to know." Woolfe explained.

"Why not?" She pressed.

"Because he thought that you would treat him the same way you do every other person that happens to pique your interest." Her friend told her.

"You know he said something similar to that earlier but I don't understand. What more could he want but me?" The Archduchess put her hands on her chest.

"I know you don't really understand the concept but he wants commitment. He wants to know that you love him and that you will only be with him." Marta explained.

"I do love him. I've loved him since we were children." She said.

"I think you're only listening to half of what I'm saying so I'll be a bit more blunt with you. He wants to marry you." Woolfe told her slightly exasperated.

"Oh, well then why didn't he just ask me? Why did he have to be all cryptic like that?" Shazaron asked.

"I suppose because he doesn't feel worthy of you or the position that he would gain if he did. About the cryptic talk perhaps he just wanted you to forget about what he said to you in the heat of battle." The wolf woman offered.

"Of all the silly things to worry about. I suppose I had better talk with him." She said.

"What are you going to do?" Her friend wondered.

"It depends upon him Marta. I'll see you later." She smiled broadly before disappearing into the crowd.

The wolf woman shrugged as she went looking for Dee and gave him a big hug when she found him. He was sitting alone with his back to a tree looking up at the stars and a large mug of elvish wine in his hand.

"Not you're normal brew." Woolfe said as she looked down at him.

"No, apparently they don't get Bridges Ale here. I think I'll remedy that as soon as I get back home." He answered, looking into the cup.

"I'm sure you will." She slid behind him as she wrapped her arms and legs around his body.

"I wasn't exactly looking for a relationship you know." He put his hand on her arm.

"Neither was I. We're just two people sharing each other's company. There's nothing wrong with that is there?" She asked.

"No I suppose there's not." He put down the Elvish wine and cuddled with her for awhile before the two of them retired for the night.

Valtarr was waiting inside the secret war room ever since his talk with Shazaron earlier that day. He was cleaning up as everyone went to the celebration but he didn't feel much like going. He told his clansmen that it was his punishment for disobeying the Archduchess whenever they asked him questions. He felt like such an idiot for confessing his true feelings to Shazaron today and he hoped that the whole matter would soon be forgotten. He sat on the cold floor alone in the dark with his arms wrapped around his legs. Feeling a little bit depressed he lightly pounded his head against the stone wall before placing it in his hands. He didn't notice the small light slowly approaching him or the soft padding of bare feet as someone entered the room.

"Still waiting for that punishment?" The cat man nearly jumped out of his skin when he heard Shazaron's voice.

"My lady." He stood up and bowed before her.

"We've known each other too long for you to be bowing before me Valtarr." She told him.

"I apologize for my disobedience earlier today and will accept any punishment you deem necessary." He did not rise from the bowing position.

"Why are you doing this when you know I have no intentions of punishing you for saving my life?" She asked him.

"If that is your wish my lady." He answered as he slowly stood up straight but he kept a downward glance.

"Valtarr, look at me." She whispered.

"Yes my lady." He looked up but his gaze didn't quite meet hers.

"I said look at me!" She demanded and her heart seemed to stop as his eyes held a deep sorrow within them.

"Yes my lady?" He wondered what she was going to do and he hoped that she wouldn't

touch him for he didn't think that he could
turn her away once more.

"What do you want from me?" She asked.

"I want nothing my lady." He told her.

"You're a terrible liar and quit being so
formal with me when you have never been that
way before." She felt a fire burn inside of
her like nothing she had ever felt before and
it was making her angry.

"I…" He bit his lower lip.

"If you don't tell me what you want then
I can't help you and I would very much like
for us to be friends again." She knelt down so
that she could be at eye level with him.

"I want you to see me as an equal." His
eyes suddenly held fire within them.

"I declared you a full member of Clan
Dameron with the rest of the trainees earlier
today." She told him.

"No, I want you to be mine and mine
alone. I want you to be my wife and I your
husband. I love you with all my heart and I
pray that you return that love to me." He
shouted as all of his emotions came out at
once.

"That's all I wanted to hear. I accept
your proposal as I have loved you since we
were children." With those words the two of
them embraced and shared a passionate kiss.

The next week was spent in bliss as the
company enjoyed the celebrations in their
honor. Mozart even teleported back to Haven's
Run to retrieve the McAllister brothers and
they all swapped stories. Falbar's quill had
to be replaced three times as he wrote down
their adventure as well as many elven songs.
He had taken quite a liking to the language
and found it to be true that most ballads

sounded better in elvish. Shazaron announced her engagement to Valtarr much to everyone's delight especially Clan Dameron. Mozart was quite frequently seen with Delatisse one of the Queen's ladies in waiting. Dee and Marta were also spending a lot of time together but by the end of the week they apparently got each other out of their systems at least for now. Clint helped Rydol restore the palace's defenses and regroup the royal guard but every night they could be seen drinking elvish wine together. It seemed that Todd and Derrkon were kind of out of place so the two of them got to know each other better and the dwarf decided that the former bandit wasn't such a bad guy after all. Martin and Vandrossa were hardly seen at all as they still had to keep their relationship a secret and since they wanted to spend as much time together as possible. They pretty much stayed in the Queen's personal area of the palace. At the end of the week all of the members of the company as well as Clan Dameron were asked to attend a special council meeting. The queen thanked them for coming and apologized once more for having to keep the siege a secret. Everyone was awarded a special Elven cloak that not only made them nearly invisible in any outdoor terrain but also gave them partial protection from any kind of attack. Then one by one the Badd Company was asked to step forward as were certain members of Clan Dameron.

"To Shadeclaw for your exceptional sacrifice I award you these blessed claws. May they protect you and help in your fight against the darkness." Vandrossa placed a set of silver claws that fit nicely over his own into his paw.

"Thank you your majesty." The tiger man bowed before her then returned to the line of his clansmen.

"To Greydon, though I did not like the way you infiltrated my city I do appreciate the sacrifice that you made for my people. There is not much I could do to restore you back the way you were perhaps this will help when it pains you." She handed him a necklace of a cat's head with a white lightning bolt on its forehead. It was hollow inside and when any kind of liquid filled it up the necklace placed a special enchantment on the fluid that when drunk alleviated any kind of pain. The grey wolf man simply bowed in silence as he returned to his friends.

"To Captain-General Marta Woolfe I give this cutlass that was once wielded by the famous elven hero Zygalfin Uthrial." She handed her the elegant weapon that was made of the finest steel and decorated with golden elven runes upon the blade.

"I am honored." The wolf woman bowed as she took the sword and stood next to her friend.

"To Todd Coalman I give you a short sword of the wolf since you seem to get along well with them." She handed him a silver sword with a wolf's head on the hilt of the weapon.

"Your majesty I do not know what to say." The man was at a loss.

"Thank you will do just fine." She smiled at him.

"Thank you." He blushed slightly as he stood next to Dee who patted him on the back.

"To Clint McAllister I give you this trench coat since you seem to like them so much." She held up a brown coat similar to the one he was wearing.

"Um no thank you your majesty I kind of like my own the best." He stated and there were many gasps of shock coming from the council and one man actually stood up but the Queen put her hand up as if telling him to be quiet.

"This 'is' your coat Clint." She smiled at him.

"What?" He looked down at his jacket in confusion.

"Mozart you can drop the illusion now." She looked at the conjurer.

"Yes your majesty." He said and as he snapped his fingers the dingy looking coat that the soldier was wearing disappeared.

"Hey!" He shouted at the elf.

"I'm sorry Clint but it was the only way I could think of to pry you away from this thing to have it enchanted for you." Vandrossa apologized.

"You could have just asked." He snorted.

"Then it wouldn't have been a surprise now would it? I thought of making it stain proof but somehow I didn't think you would appreciate that so instead I made it immune to fire, acid, and a few other things that might destroy it." She held up the trench coat with the blood stains before him and he took it happily.

"Thanks Sh…I mean your majesty." He bowed slightly and put the coat on as he stepped back next to his comrades.

"To Falbar Teroth I give you this lute that once belonged to Gilhalfel Lynin a great Elven bard and her feather quill. May it never run out of ink" She gave him a hand carved lute that depicted a minstrel singing to a group of angels and a white feather quill.

"Your majesty?" He looked at her curiously.

"The quill can write without ink and if you make a mistake you can erase it with this." She pulled the end out of the feather to reveal a flat rubber thing on the inside.

"Thank you your majesty." He bowed before her excited at his new prize.

"To Mozart Martakamis I give to you the sorcerer's robes of Shadreth Talani who shared your taste in wardrobe." She handed him a long purple garment that had elegant golden designs around the shoulders and neck.

"I am greatly honored. Thank you your majesty." He had heard of the powerful sorcerer and stories of his great works were still shared in the school that he had gone to which was the very same one that Mozart graduated from in Clennross.

"To Derrkon Rockbeard I give to you a necklace of Bargovin. May it always inspire you to create great things." She handed the dwarf a golden necklace with a Mithril anvil hanging from it.

"Thank you your majesty." He bowed to her before returning to his comrades.

"To Martin Tierleaf I give you Willamina's ring. She too was a servant of The Bright One and the ring is said to have strange powers for their servants." She hated to use his unmarried name but it was necessary.

"Thank you your majesty I will do my best to honor her memory." He took the simple golden ring from her but when he withdrew his hand she stopped him.

"I'm not quite through with you. The Vugakut has given you the title of Puveg which is a bishop for those of you that do not know our titles. He is here to give you your new collar." She stepped back to allow the Elven priest to approach and Martin knelt down before him.

"For your great service to Plenty and to The Bright One you are honored with the rank of Puveg." The Vugakut or High Patriarch took off Martin's old white collar and placed a new one with a yellow stripe on top of it around his neck.

"I accept this title and will do my best to continue my services to The Bright One and to the nation of Plenty." Martin bowed before the High Patriarch and the Queen and then returned to the line of his friends.

"To Captain Rydol Oaktree I give you the guardian sword and the council has accepted you as one of its members." She handed him a beautiful elven sword with matching runes on the blade and the symbol of Sonya on the pommel.

"I am always at your service your majesty and I am honored to be counted as one of your councilmen." He took the sword, bowed, and then sat at the great table with his fellow councilors.

"To Valanche Dee Bridges I give to you the transformation device. For now you can use it to replace your lost short sword but it can become any metal object that you might need." She gave him a short sword that seemed to shine and shimmer.

"Thank you your majesty." He smiled at her as he took the weapon.

"To Archduchess Shazaron Dameron who was named elf friend I give to you this ring. It will forever assure you safe passage through the forests of Plenty and guard you against evil." She handed her a golden ring encrusted

with a large ruby and on the ruby was a golden
Arden tree.

"Thank you your majesty." The two women
bowed to each other and then they hugged one
another fondly.

After Shazaron had rejoined the others,
the Queen addressed the room once more. "These
heroes are to be honored in the city of
Clinton and though their great deeds in Plenty
cannot be known at present they will forever
be remembered." Vandrossa and the entire
council bowed before the lines of people
standing before them.

"And now your majesty we can address more
important matters." A dark haired male elf
that was sitting at the grand table stood up.

"I see it is always business with you
Lord Orrenthal." The Queen gestured for the
heroes to be seated.

"And it is grave business indeed your
majesty." The Elven noble spoke with disdain
in his voice.

"What business could there possibly be to
speak about now Lord Orrenthal?" A blonde
haired elven woman spoke up.

"Why the Queen's betrayal Lady Myrinna."
The nobleman turned to face her.

"What evil do you speak!?" A dark haired
elven woman demanded.

"Not evil but truth, the Queen has
committed adultery with the most foul of
beasts, a deep elf." He pointed at Vandrossa
as he looked at the other councilors.

"Liar!" One woman shouted.

"Foul snake!" Another woman cursed and
the room erupted in argument.

"I have proof, confessions from the very
mouth of the one she was with." The noble
nodded and two elven guardsmen opened up a

side door and four other guards walked in to the chambers dragging a white haired, grey skinned elf.

Vandrossa's insides shook with fear and Martin had to be held back by Dee to keep him from doing anything. The half-elf tried to contain his anger but it could clearly be seen in his eyes as he stared at the creature that had violated his wife.

"We cannot trust the word of that monstrosity." Lady Myrinna calmly stated.

"The High Patriarch could tell us if he speaks falsely." Lord Orrenthal offered.

"He does not need to. Lord Orrenthal speaks the truth." The Queen admitted.

"You see, she has not yet been married long enough to produce an heir and she betrays our King with this foul beast." The room again erupted in argument.

"That's not fair to accuse the Queen when you do not know the whole story." Dee stood up and walked over to the nobleman.

"Who are you to address this council?" The elf demanded.

"I'm Lord Dee Bridges as you well know." He answered.

"I know your name but it means nothing when dealing with council matters." The elf dismissed the man.

"It does when you're too arrogant or too stupid to hear the whole truth. The Queen was enchanted by a powerful wizard when she tried to escape the city!" Synbadd was starting to get angry.

"You will hold your tongue sir or I'll have it cut out!" He pointed angrily at the nobleman.

"Lord Orrenthal I represent this man and he speaks for me!" Rydol stood up.

"Then you will do well to teach him some manners before he addresses a member of this council." The elf stared at the soldier.

"Why don't you ask the Vugakut to Divinate on behalf of the Queen? I'm sure that he will be shown the truth of my words. I'm sure that he will see a wizard casting a spell upon her and then forcing her to this act. I'm also sure that he will see that Falanna herself forgave the Queen and cleansed her in a holy spring so that she could be free of the wrong that was done to her." As Dee spoke the Queen became reassured that she was forgiven and purified making her free of any sin yet she was slightly embarrassed that he knew so much.

"So you've said before. Do you honestly think that I or this council should believe that Sket Roan dominated the Queen to betray her husband with that foul beast?" He crossed his arms over his chest.

At the words Sket Roan Martin's fury reached its peak and both Clint and Mozart had to hold him in place. They couldn't allow their friend to blow his cover as the councilman unwittingly just did when he told everyone who it was that was behind the violation to the queen.

"Lord Orrenthal I do not believe that I named the wizard that enchanted the Queen nor did I say what spell was used. How is it that you know?" Dee looked at the noble, triumphant.

"I, well, who else could it have been? It is a well known fact that you are his enemies." He fumbled for words to turn it back around on Synbadd but no one was with him at this point.

"Guards, arrest Lord Orrenthal and find out what else he knows!" Vandrossa finally spoke up.

"You are making a grave mistake! It is the Queen you should be punishing not me. She's the betrayer to this country not me! Not me!" He shouted as the guards surrounded him.

"No Lord Orrenthal it is you that have made a mistake and you will be paying for that with your very life." The Queen told him as he was being led out.

"You will pay! You will all pay! No one can stand in his way!" He was shouting nonsensically after that and the council stood in silence for a short while after the nobleman was led out of the room.

"Are you alright your majesty?" Rydol asked concerned because of the damage that Lord Orrenthal's words may have caused.

"Yes Rydol I am fine." She smiled at him then fainted.

The captain was barely able to catch her and the whole room seemed to run towards her. It was Martin that finally picked her up and took her out of the room with the High Patriarch and a few others following them. The council was in an uproar at the events that unfolded before them and in the end they needed to break so that they could discuss things on their own.

Chapter 11
"Deceptions"

Vandrossa awoke in familiar surroundings as she sat up in her own bed and found that she was alone. She wanted to get up to look for whoever brought her here but she was still feeling light headed. Tired, she decided to just lie back down and wait for someone to check on her. Two minutes later the door to her room swung open as two individuals walked inside. Martin was the first one through the door and when he saw that his wife was awake he was instantly at her side.

"Vandrossa my love, how are you feeling?" He grabbed her hand and kissed it softly.

"Tired, what happened?" She asked weakly.

"You fainted." He answered her.

"No, I mean with the council." She clarified.

"Oh well…" He was cut short.

"They dismissed everyone and reconvened in private." A 5' tall brown haired elf with green eyes and wearing the white robes of a servant of The Bright One spoke up.

"Drava, you should be with them in my stead." The queen looked at him sternly.

"I would your majesty but your health is more important. Don't worry they are not without spiritual guidance. High Kluset Arriallina is taking my place. She is very wise and will someday inherit my mantle." The priest informed her.

"No one could ever take your place Drava." She smiled at him.

"Thank you for saying so your majesty" He bowed slightly.

"So what is ailing me?" Vandrossa glanced at the two men. Martin looked up at the High

Patriarch who just nodded to him so he turned back to his wife.

"You are with child my love." He told her.

"No." She whispered softly.

"Two actually" Drava said.

"Is it…?" She couldn't even ask for fear of the answer.

"You needn't worry my love the babies are mine." Martin put one arm behind her head and the other on her stomach and pulled her towards him.

"Thank The Bright One." She sighed in relief as she embraced her husband and put her head on his chest.

"Yes, thank The Bright One but we need to discuss what is to be announced to the council." The High Patriarch said.

"What do you mean?" The Queen wondered.

"One conspirator has been uncovered but do you really think that Lord Orrenthal was acting alone?" He looked at her with concern.

"No I do not." She went limp in her husband's arms.

"Vandrossa?" Martin was worried that she had fainted once more.

"I don't suppose Lord Orrenthal was any help in finding out who else is working with Sket." She stated flatly.

"No, he is suffering from some kind of curse or madness and I have yet to restore his mind to him. Hopefully he was an unwilling participant but I fear that it is not the case because he allowed the enchantment to effect him." Drava explained.

"I see." She sat up and looked down at her feet.

"Even if the curse is removed he may not
know anything that could help us reveal all of
the traitors in our midst." He continued.

"Which means that Martin and our future
children are in grave danger. Drava why do you
suppose I'm still safe here?" Vandrossa asked
as she looked into her husband's eyes.

"Perhaps because whoever is behind this
does not control enough of the council to
place them in charge if you are killed." He
answered.

"In that case would you be willing to
keep one more secret Drava?" She asked.

"You want me to keep your pregnancy
confidential?" The priest already knew what
she needed.

"No, that is a secret that we couldn't
keep for long besides I wouldn't want to
jeopardize their birthright. I just want the
fact that my future children are Martin's
hidden from the council. We need to allow Sket
and his conspirators to think that their evil
deed produced an illegitimate heir." She
grabbed her husband's hand and he squeezed it
in support.

"I cannot announce that you are to bear
the child of a deep elf for it would go badly
for all concerned especially when they are
born. The council will either demand that I be
removed from my position or your enemies could
claim that you are lying and the children
belong to someone else." He was truly
concerned for the future of the kingdom.

"No, I would not have you say that but
you could claim that your vision is clouded by
The Bright One and that you are unsure of who
the father is until the babies are born. This
would protect every one until it is safe for
all to be revealed and hopefully the

opposition will see this as a sign that they have won this small victory." The queen hated all the dishonesty that had surrounded her from childhood but it has been necessary to keep her and her family alive.

"I think that The Bright One would approve of this small deception in order to preserve your family's lives. Would you like for me to speak with the council now or do you wish to address them yourself?" Drava asked.

"It would be best if you spoke to them right now. I'm still very tired from the past few events and I need to speak to my husband in private." She smiled weakly at the High Patriarch.

"As you wish my lady" He bowed before departing the Queen's room.

"What is it you need to speak to me about my love?" Martin asked after the priest closed the door behind him.

"You need to go back to Haven's Run with Dee." She looked deep into his eyes.

"No I can't leave you like this." He dropped to his knees and grabbed her hands.

"You must go Martin. It is still dangerous for you to be here." Tears streamed down both of their faces.

"I'm willing to risk it; I cannot allow you to bear this burden alone." He wrapped his arms around her and buried his face in her bosom.

"I'm sorry Martin but it is for our children's sake as well as yours. If Sket's servants aren't found by the time they are born they will need a place to hide and you would be the only one that could protect them." She held her husband and he squeezed her tighter for support.

"I know, it hurts me just as much you to be parted from you like this again. We've had so little time to be together and my heart aches for this to be finally over." Fresh tears streamed down his face as he looked at her.

"Perhaps it would have been better if we never met at all. I have brought you nothing but hardship." She got up and walked towards a large window to look outside.

"No my beloved I love you and I would rather spend one lifetime in hardship with you then to spend a thousand lifetimes in bliss without you." He stood behind her and held her in his arms.

"I love you so much Martin. Thank you for all that you have given me. You have made me strong enough to endure and do what I have to." She turned around to return her husband's embrace.

"Then I shall be strong as well and return with Dee to Haven's Run. You are right, so long as Sket has power here we will not be safe nor will our children. If you need me for any reason promise that you will tell me right away and I will have Mozart teleport me to you, alright?" He held her head up and stared into her eyes.

"I promise. Are you sure that I'm carrying your children?" She asked feeling a little guilty for her insecurity.

"Yes my love. I have seen them; one boy and one girl." He smiled at her as he brushed her cheek.

"What do they look like?" She asked.

"The boy looks just like me with your lovely green eyes and the girl has your strength. She will be as beautiful as you with stunning blue eyes and she will have a royal grace that will make the people love her." He spoke with pride.

"Stay with me tonight?" The queen asked hopefully.

"Nothing could make me do otherwise." He bent down and kissed her fervently.

The company waited for several hours as the council deliberated and the Queen was taken away. They were worried that something horrible was going on and they hoped that their new found friend was alright. The High Patriarch soon showed up to tell the company that Vandrossa was fine and that they could visit her as soon as she felt well enough to walk about. Then for some reason he asked Dee if he would join him in the council chambers and he quickly agreed. So while the company was escorted by a few guards to the royal quarters Synbadd accompanied Drava into the council chambers.

"Lord Kalrin you were seen on a number of occasions speaking to Lord Orrenthal away from prying ears." A blonde haired elven man accused.

"As were you Lord Falkeys; as were many of us." An elven woman spoke up.

"Councilmen please we should not be fighting amongst ourselves not now that our Queen and our country need us the most. A great evil has been vanquished and we should be celebrating not causing more strife." A tall black haired elf spoke and there was much approval at his words.

"Lord Sylro speaks the truth. Do not allow the traitor Orrenthal to divide us for the good of the people." A beautiful blonde haired elven woman supported his words.

"Vugakut how fairs the Queen?" Rydol
noticed the priest and all eyes were upon him.

"The Queen is well Captain." He bowed
slightly.

"What ails her?" A brown haired elven
woman dressed in the white robes of The Bright
One asked.

"Nothing, the queen is with child
Arriallina." He informed the council.

"And who is the father?" A noblewoman
asked.

"I'm not sure. My vision has been clouded
and I do not know if the child is the result
of the attack on the Queen." He lied.

"Then it is possible that she is to bear
an illegitimate child?" One of the nobles
wondered.

"I do not know." The priest answered.

"This is disturbing news." Lady Myrinna
hung her head.

"What is he doing here? This is a closed
council meeting." The blonde elven woman
demanded.

"He is here at my request Lady
Illinvanna." He told her.

"For what purpose?" She asked.

"Lady Illinvanna the Vugakut can invite
whoever he wishes to any council meeting
closed or not without permission from anyone
as you well know." High Kluset Arriallina
informed the irate woman.

"Enough of this useless banter! Drava,
were you able to find out anything from Lord
Orrenthal?" Lord Falkeys was more interested
in the traitor than the human that the priest
brought with him.

"No unfortunately he is under a powerful
curse and it may be some time before I can
remove it from him but I fear that will do us

no good. He was just a pawn in the plot to destroy our kingdom and he probably knows very little." The priest informed the council.

"Figures." The nobleman crossed his arms across his chest.

"Now Lord Falkeys you should not be angry with the Vugakut and we should not be so eager to pass judgment on Lord Orrenthal. If he is a victim of this whole evil business then he should have our pity not our anger." Lord Sylro looked at the man and he lowered his head as if ashamed.

"Lord Sylro is correct. There is nothing that we could do right now but wait to see what Orrenthal has to say after Drava cures him. For now we should adjourn and show our Queen our support." Lady Myrinna stated.

"And so we shall. This council is adjourned." A black haired elf announced and the council slowly departed.

"Drava…" Rydol was going to ask him a question but the priest stopped him.

"Come with me Rydol and you as well Lord Bridges." Drava looked at them and they both nodded in approval.

The High Patriarch led them through the palace chapel to a small room where he gestured for the two men to sit down. He cast a few spells before he sat down in front of them.

"What we are about to discuss should not leave this room." He spoke to them seriously.

"Is the Queen truly alright?" Rydol was worried.

"Yes and because the both of you are trusted with all of her secrets you should know that she carries Martin's children." He told them.

"Children?" Rydol was curious at his words.

"She is to have twins and she will need your help especially you Rydol. Twins are not easy for any Elven woman to bear especially when her husband cannot be with her." He said.

"Of course, so why did you have Lord Bridges come with you to the council meeting?" The soldier wondered.

"To get an outside opinion" He looked at Synbadd and continued. "What did you think Lord Bridges?" He turned to face the nobleman.

"The Queen has many enemies within the council." Synbadd said.

"What? Who?" Rydol was shocked.

"Lord Falkeys, Lady Illinvanna, to name a few and I think that they're being led by Lord Sylro." He stated flatly.

"That cannot be." The soldier shook his head.

"I believe Lord Bridges is correct. They seem to be the ones that are most against the Queen although I'm not so sure about Lord Sylro." Drava said.

"Neither am I. He has always loved the Queen." Rydol protested.

"That only makes him more dangerous. Does he know about Martin?" Dee wondered.

"No one in the council knows who the king is because his life was threatened before he married the Queen." The soldier informed the man.

"If that's the case, then why is Martin hunted by assassins?" The nobleman wondered.

"Well he was publicly courting her but when the assassins started to appear it was announced that their engagement was broken. Someone probably suspects that was a just a ruse to protect him." The priest offered.

"Yeah that sounds very likely." Synbadd nodded in agreement.

"Why do you suspect Lord Sylro?" Rydol wondered.

"Because of how much he tries to look like the good guy. He says things that support the Queen and appears genuine but he sits back and smiles when anything is said to go against her. He looks like a snake in the grass waiting to attack his prey and if I were you I would keep a close watch on Lady Myrinna as well." He spoke his opinion.

"There is no way in Avaria that she's a conspirator." Rydol protested.

"No I don't believe that she is but she's an obvious thorn in their side and they may try to have her removed from office or even killed." The nobleman told them.

"You may be right Lord Bridges. Rydol you should have a few of the secret guard protect her but don't let anyone know that you have." Drava ordered.

"Yes your grace." He bowed slightly.

"Thank you Lord Bridges, sometimes an outsider can see what we are too blind to notice. We shall definitely keep a close watch on Lord Sylro from now on." The priest shook his hand and Rydol nodded in approval.

Later that evening the company discussed what had happened with the Queen and the council. They all agreed that Sket had a definite influence in Plenty and that their friend Martin was not safe here. Most privately swore to protect their friend and help him to become stronger so that one day he may return without fear. The next day they bid the queen and Rydol a fond farewell before teleporting back to Haven's Run. All except

Shazaron and Marta who chose to travel back
with the members of Clan Dameron.

After all of the great heroes left the
city a shadow quickly ran from the palace and
slipped into an abandoned house deep within
the forest. The figure pulled out a red
crystal and spoke the magic words that would
activate the device.

"High Magus, we regret to inform you that
the capital of Plenty is no longer in our
control." The man spoke into the crystal.

"Did you get the scrolls that I asked you
for?" An evil voice replied.

"Yes but I'm not sure if they're the ones
you've been looking for." He answered.

"Send them to me Falkeys and I will tell
you if they are the ones." The voice ordered.

"Yes Lord Sket." The nobleman said before
he started to conjure and the scroll that he
carried disappeared out of his hands.

"At last the final location of the great
Black Diamond of Elfindorial is within my
grasp. You have done well Lord Falkeys." The
High Magus crooned.

"What of my reward?" The elf wondered.
"You shall have your reward Lord Falkeys.
Ezulock!" Sket shouted and the crystal in the
nobleman's hands blew up killing him
instantly. The High Magus smiled wickedly at
his triumph for at last he had found the clue
that would bring him absolute power over all.
Plenty can have their little victory for now
but it won't last long Sket thought as he
turned to more important matters. It was the
calm before the storm and the Badd Company
would soon feel his wrath.